MURPHY ON THE MOUNT

David Justice

I0684882

Lingua Sacra Publishing

Murphy On The Mount
Copyright © 2010 by David Justice

Published in the United States by Lingua Sacra
Publishing.
www.linguasacrapublishing.com
ISBN 978-0-9843432-3-2

Dedication

To my beloved bride for over thirty years.

Acknowledgements

With appreciation for all the people at Lingua Sacra Publishing, especially Keith Massey, Editor-in-Chief and friend.

About the Author

David Justice, Ph.D., is the author of *The Semantics of Form in Arabic* and a collection of short stories about the Murphy Brothers, *I Don't Do Divorce Cases*. He was editor of Etymology and Pronunciation at Merriam-Webster, and Editor-in-Chief at Franklin Electronic Publishers. His short stories have appeared in *Ellery Queen* and *Alfred Hitchcock's Mystery Magazine*. He is currently working as a linguist. To read selected stories from *I Don't Do Divorce Cases* and new short fiction visit his blog at: http://murphybros.blogspot.com/

Murphy on the Mount

"De l'audace, encore de l'audace -- toujours de l'audace!"

-- Casey Stengel (often wrongly attributed to General Patton, Friedrich der Grosse, or Danton)

Pre-Vision

I walk slowly up the long and narrow street, which seems to narrow further as I go. For there is no-one, no-one; deserted since the beginning of time. I stop and listen: alone, with nobody but the wind. I look at the high walls around me and they're not even vandalized, any graffiti long since flaked away. It's like — I stop: feeling shaky. It's like being all alone on a beach, some beach you never been to, only — you've been there, you've been here, in your dreams, or in another life, or just last week but you have amnesia. This dead end, this empty air-pocket in what used to be, in better days, the wrong part of town. And which now is the left lane of nowhere, only reckoned to lie within the city limits by convention of topography. No-one walks these sidewalks, no-one sweeps these streets — which yet are littered with losing racetrack stubs, unsent mash notes, candy-wrappers from discontinued candies, blown in from some other continent. The wind whistles down the main drag westways, and then the earth tilts and it whistles back on the other tack. It is like the long and stretching sands, back when the sun stared down with red-blind Cyclops eye on the primitive landscape, before we even evolved, before the first baffled-stranded fish crawled up (gasping) out of the sea.

And I am swaying here, I could disappear, the sea would creep up and all would vanish. I turn, and turn, searching for some sign that anyone has ever been here. And up a ways, on the other side, a single sheet of newspaper blows: now rising, now sinking and sighing, and rising again. Could this be a clue? But it won't be yesterday's: some other town perhaps, in some other language from some other century, minus a headline, minus a by-line, just been blowing around and around this old earth, up in the jet stream, for years and years, and now settling down here.

Chapter One

So one June, one afternoon, we're sitting around and I say: "You know what I think, Joey?"

"What do you think, Murphy."

"I think we need a secretary."

He looks at me like my strait-jacket's slipped, he's thinking I bust outa my bin. "A *secretary*? Murphy we got no *customers*, whadawe need a secretary for?"

"You know, some slick broad, class up the front office, handle our calls."

"Murphy Murphy, nobody *calls* us. The front office, that's just the front a *this* office, the place where the beds fold up durina day. We don't got but one room!"

"Not counting the pool room," I astutely note.

"Dang right I'm not countina pool room, whacha gonna do, yagonna put 'er in *there*? In back? Plus first you know you'd hafta move out that moose head, Murphy —"

"Oh don't get on to me about that moose head again."

"An 'en all them *pizza* boxes, all piled up, like it's a tower to heaven —"

"It is, it is! 'Smatta wichoo, you never played with blocks?"

"An 'en-a *tires*, Murphy, o-o-o-o-o-oh, the tires ...."

"Yeh well you know how it is."

"That I do, Murphy, that I do. Other guys pick up stray cats or stray diseases; you, you pick up stray tires."

"You know it, Joey. Tires what had no home."

"I know it, Murphy. I'm not knocking your tires."

"They're nice tires."

"The best — in their day. But just — *Mu-u-ur-r-phy*...."

And right then — bingo — a knock at the door.

"Now see what I mean, Joey? A customer! Don't you wish we had a secretary right now? She could deal with 'em while we hide in back, say we're too busy, say that we died."

"C'mon, Murphy, party's gonna get tired knocking. Opena door."

"You open it. Makes me nervous, customers."

Joey opens it and — Ooh, Wah, Doo: a customer — and what a customer! It's a dame, — but that don't describe it. I mean, your *mother's* a dame, if it comes to that. No I mean like, a *da-a-ame* dame: with everything on it. She got shiny hair, so clear you could shave your face in it. She got lips like a paint sale. She got teeth, make a dentist say: I'm ready, Lord, I seen it all, you can take me now. She got eyes like ice, and it ain't melting. A neck, would make the Boston Strangler just throw up his hands, he wouldn't hardly know where to begin. Then a blouse, a white blouse, the front part of it all scooped out, like a dish of ice cream. And below, oh, the double dip, I'm peeking through my fingers; and her waist is like a sugar cone. Then all that flesh that was left over from the middle, they just slabbed it onto the hips with a trowel. And then she goes and tapers down again, she's like a spinning top, you'd a think she'd fall over, just these slim little feet and tall high heels and the shoes come to a point like a kick-knife.

"You a shamus?" she says, looking at Joey.

He blushes and mumbles, "Me an' him."

She looks me over, half her mouth does this little stab at a smile. "You'll do." And I think: You too.

I tip the beer-cans off the chair and offer it to her like a gentleman. With a ladylike swish, she sits down. I sit down on the crate, and Joey sort of edges off to the kitchen part of the room.

"I got a job for you," she says.

"Well we're pretty busy, but I guess I can fit in you, I mean fit you in."

I think I maybe I see an eyebrow budge, but not much. "*You* ? — b-*busy*??!!" she says. — I don't like the tone.

I match it. "Yeh, we was thinkina doin' our nails."

Definitely a rise of an eyebrow this time. I think.

"It's like this, shamus. There's a fellow that I want to see him dead."

Oh no not again. Why, why, does this keep happening to me? I sort of get off the crate real slow.

"Listen, sister: maybe we're hungry but we're not just from hunger. We'd be eating the last little leavings outa the garbage can what the *wino* left behind, and we still not be up for *that*. You come to the wrong address."

"Can it, shamus. There's just a guy that I want you to find him, is all — dead or alive, though dead would suit me just dandy."

"Hm, well, we usually like our clients alive."

She glares at me and snaps: "*He's* not your client — *I* am!"

Joey and I make these little O's with our mouths, and look at each other and shake our heads.

"Well now that remains to be seen, and me I ain't seein' it," I say, "'cause you was just leavin'."

"Yeh," says Joey, opening the door, "we're real sorry you coulden stay."

She stands up fast, eyes sending out sparks, kind of quivering, but then — some little tendon somewhere snaps, she starts twisting her handbag, and the ice in her eyes turns to slush. "I'm — sorry. I snapped at you. If you'll hear me out, you'll see why I'm so tense."

Again the glance-exchange with Joey, but this time no O's.

"An apology!" I comment.

He nods concurrence. "An actual apology."

"Don't meet many o' those things round hereabouts, *these* days, bro'."

"Darn for sure: they be — thin on the ground."

"Ahh! that magic word, 'Sorry', that makes things all better. — Okay sister, take a seat, I reckon you can find it yourself this time."

She found it all right.

"So okay, so how's about you tell us in your own words what happen. Who is this guy?"

"My husband — my *ex*, if I have anything to do with it."

Dang. Not again. "Lady — really sorry — but — we don't do divorce cases."

Impatient. "He walked out on me. Not much left to divorce. Just hear me out, okay? Later for the scruples."

"All right, all right." I get businesslike, like. "So how'd you meet this guy, when he was still your *to-be*?"

"I was working in a travel agency at the time — Willie's Worldwide Travel, downtown. Richie was a steady customer, always flying off to places like Zurich, the Cayman Islands, Rome, Naples, Corsica — really sent me back to the geography books sometimes. I didn't fall so much in love with *him* as with the places he was always going off to — not even the places, really, since I never seen a one of them, but just like the *idea* of the places, the *names*."

We maintained a respectful silence, and she went on.

"Willie my boss was a prize flagpole. All day yakking on the phone, not work stuff either, stuff with his hobby, which was breeding dogs. Like we don't already got enough dogs. Never did a lick of work otherwise. But he knew people, they came in. I think he knew Richie from before. But they weren't close — he still let me handle Richie's reservations. And what reservations — first class all the way.

"I'm just the girl there, you know, but one time, it's about the tenth time I'm booking him a flight, and I been learning about his tastes and all, what he chooses in a hotel, and ecsetera like that. And now Willie's out somewhere and I'm alone with him in the office, so I ask him, flirting a little, is it *business or pleasure*. And he gives me this — *dreamy* smile, I mean not like he was dreaming but just this soft shy elegant dignified hint of a smile, and he murmurs: 'A little of both.'

"That did it for me. I must of blushed. Anyway he laughed and said, 'You're quite a girl.' And I said, 'I am?', and he said 'You are!' and I said, 'Really?' — and the sunlight's streaking in through the little windows that they could use some washing and bouncing off his gold watch and from my sighing eyes I'm watching and it's like the brightest object in the room. Maybe except for his smile. Then he says, 'And it might be a pleasure, doing business with you.'

"Now normally I don't allow a gentleman says something like that to a girl, girl's got her reputation to look out for; but he gives me this big smile and his teeth are *perfect*, and I'm thinking: This can't be happening to me. He's obviously loaded, always pays cash, just peeling off these crisp hundred-dollar bills, fwip fwip fwip, from a wad as big and long and round as a, as an I don't know what. 'Yes,' he says, 'You - are - *quite — a — gal* ....' And I sigh and I say, 'Do you really think so?', not even caring am I being too forward for a nice girl like me brought up right with a reputation to protect because the music of his words and the dream of his smile and at this point I am willing to risk all —"

"Hey, could we cut to the chase a little?" breaks in Joey. "Save all that for the weepie magazines. Think I'm gonna lose my lunch."

"*Anyway*," glaring, "he asks me out, says we'll have dinner in Paris and do I have any favorite places there, well I quit my job right then and there, leaving a nasty note for Willie on his computer screen and go out flipping the sign around so it says 'Sorry We Missed You — CLOSED'.

"And then, well, something comes up and we don't go to Paris, but we go to my apartment, and you can guess the rest. And then I'm crying, and he's laughing and he's stroking my hair, and he's calling me 'Silly thing' but in a nice way, and it's getting to me, yes, it is getting to me, *getting* to me, yes, yes it is; and I put my arms round him and I draw him down, down to me, down down down *down* to me; *yes* and he murmuring (Yes! and I — murmuring he) asks, *Will you marry me?,* and I say (Yes!), I say Yes — yes — yes yes *yes yes* **yes**."

" 'Yes'; right. We heard you the first time." Joey all sour, like he been weaned on a pickle.

7

"We just go and get married quick at the registry because he has this incredibly important business trip, he's gonna buy us a house with what he makes on it, but he promises a round-the-world honeymoon soon — *not* through Willie's Worldwide," a bitter smile, "and then house-hunting."

"And then maybe you got time, you get married the *right* way," says Joey grimly. "In a church."

She doesn't notice. "He says he wants to keep me in style — in a style I'm unaccustomed to — and I shall never want for anything." Even with all that later happened, she sighs at the memory.

"Guess you had ta be there," Joey mutters.

"He says we should have a joint bank account — share and share alike! Only his is so large, really *large*, that he can't move it over without interest penalties and things, so instead we add his name to mine. I've been tucking away what I can, living pretty simply so it's finally come up to something, and he's going to add to it out of the profits of his trip, soon's he gets back. And I say Darling, you are too good to me, and I embrace him, my white arms flung round his deep-tanned manly neck —"

Joey starts leafing through a magazine.

"— and he laughs and then he gets passionate all over again, myself again feeling, and deeply a woman; and we have quite a time of it until alas it is time for him to leave."

I nod. Don't like where this is going.

"That was two weeks ago. A week later he's still not back, and then I get a notice from my bank that my check has bounced. A five-dollar check! So I go in to see what is this, and they tell me my account has been cleaned out, what, didn't I know; just only not *closed* out, because that requires both signatures. Then I go back to my apartment and some other things are missing, things I'm really gonna miss, and I realize I've been had. And had good."

Nodding, frowning. "So you come straight to us."

"Not right away. I still couldn't believe it. Some — crazy mistake, or ... I mean he never acted shifty or anything, if he's really a bad actor then he's a really good actor. But another week goes by and no call, not even a post card, so I finally say, Girl, that does it; and I come to you."

Okay; check. "So how you find out about us? Been talking to one of our many satisfied customers?"

A shrug. "You were in the phone book, the only listing with no ad and no bold-face or nothing, just a number and a name. So I figured you were cheap. I mean — he took everything."

"Hmm. Cheap is as cheap does. So how much you were figuring you could afford?"

"Well ... What are your usual rates?"

I look over to Joey. Gimme a figure! What do I know? But before he can say anything, she says:

"It doesn't matter anyway — Richie cleaned me out. I'll have to pay you when you find him — brother, I'll make him pay! And if he's dead, then I'll inherit, then I'll be rolling in it, and you can name your price."

"Mm. Hunh. Just a moment while I consult with my colleague."

We step back into the pool room and close the door.

"This is worse than Wimpy," says Joey. "'I will gladly pay you Tuesday for a hamburger today', only in the meantime you have to find me the money."

"Which we are to get —"

"— from her worst enemy, a con man slippery as an eel —"

"— who is probably by now in another country —"

"— what we don't even know what country it is. Which *hemisphere*."

"Does not look good."

"That it does not."

"Bad."

"Very bad."

"But on the other hand —"

"— we know what beggars can't be."

"She's on."

"She's on."

We go back in, looking grave.

"Good news, madam. Owing to certain unusual features of interest, we have decided to take your case."

The dame already looks bored. "Imagine my relief."

I whip out an envelope what the back is not been written on yet, wet the end of a pencil, and get down to cases.

"Okay, for starters. Your name?"

"Do you really need that?"

I look up from the envelope (some unpaid bill), dismayed at how this case hits a brick wall before it's even up and running. "Lady lady, you give us no money, no name, you forget to say Please and Thank you — what if we forget we're working for you? *Names*, lady; it's the done thing."

"Alright. Alright. It's LaBelle."

"LaBelle, LaBelle. Hum it for me, wouldja? Is that like Mary LaBelle or like LaBelle P. Smith?"

"LaBelle LeBaron."

"Whooh! Okay, whatever you say. And the disappeared party. Richie LeBaron? Richie Le-What?"

"No, just Richie Mallow. I kept my own name."

"Lady, it was me, I was you, I'd'a taken his moniker just to get shut of one or two a them *L*s. But I guess since he skipped out on ya, you're just as glad you didn't cop his handle. Anyhow. Anyways. Where was I. No — where was *he*. Where was he heading, when he left on his trip?"

"How shd'*eye* know? *You're* the P.I. He takes off, okay? Rio, Montreal, Berlin, this and this and that. He never told me about his business stuff."

"Well I thought you mighta maybe drove him to the airport." Anything, anything for a clue.

11

"No — matter of fact, I offered to, us being married and all, though just for a few days. But he wasn't having any."

"Hm. Yeh. Case like that, we had one once, back in Shanghai. Didn't turn out too good, though. — So like just what business was he in."

"I already toleja, I don't know. *Stuff*. I didn't care, so long as he was flush. That was pretty much his attitude too. Didn't like for people to be breathing down his neck. So like — don't neither you breathe down on mine."

I ignored the jab. "I'm getting the picture. You were pretty trusting, in a way."

"Don't I bloody know it. But from now on I'm locking my door, believe you me. I even bought a police lock with what I had left in my handbag. And if he tries to come back, his key won't fit."

"Little late for that, right? Horse gone, barn door?"

"Nothing more to steal, if that's what you're getting at. But he might want to drop by sometime and sort of slip in and assert his conjugal rights. Or ice me to keep me from going to the cops."

"But you haven't gone to the cops."

"No, they make me allergic. And what do they care? I don't even know if he did anything illegal. I mean we were married, and it was a joint account."

"The jewels weren't joint, though."

"Howja know it was jewels?"

12

"I'm a detective, right? Little grey cells. You said he took some other stuff. He's leaving by plane, looks like, so it's a cinch he didn't take your back issues of *Cosmopolitan* or your car."

"Yeh, right; had an eye for it, too. The good piece he took; the paste he let be."

"So okay, so we're getting somewhere. So he knows that there is nothing more to take. I don't think he'll be back. Plus he sounds like the kind of actor can get a piece of ... can get some conjugal action going, whenever he wants — Hey don't take offense, I'm just telling you you can sleep easy. And listen — he's not going to ice you now, thinking you might squawk — you'd'a squawked, you'd'a squawked by now. Guys who ice guys, ice 'em quick, or not at all. And you're right, there's not much to nail him on as yet; give it a few more weeks you can claim desertion, is all. No really, a guy like that, planes and janes and flights and fine wines, he isn't going to bother go around icing guys, just because they might kaffeeklatsch his little misdeeds — he'd be in the wrong business. Him I reckon went wrong long ago. Probably back in pre-school. Borrowed a bunny book from the library and never gave it back. He still has it, he owes now ninety-nine thousand dollars in fines, compound interest, but he's just laughing — laughing and laughing; and all the children there in nursery school, they're all crying and crying, *O NOoes, we wants our Bunny Book* — but he just sneers and lights up another cigar. — O yes oh yes,

13

I know his type, got it taped, got it nailed; you're well rid of him sister. He walked out on you — best goddamn day of your life. Oughta celebrate — hoist a Coke or something.

"But still. Hey. You got it, use the lock now you've got it. Keeps the cops out in any case, what's-not-to-like. Cause him, he's off and gone; but a guy like that, he might know some guys, some guys that have friends, kind you don't want to have over for bridge."

She seemed a bit baffled by all this, but said: "Will do."

"Okay. Right. Okay." Little check-mark with the pencil. "Anything else you can tell us. Like — Age?"

"Of all the nerve!"

"*His* age, sister, *he's* the guy we're looking for. And a photograph, if we can trouble you and interrupt your reverie."

Indignant, but she tamps it down. "Maybe forty. Oh … thirty-nine-and-a-half."

Joey rolled his eyes.

"But no photos. Like I said, we got hitched at the registry, quick. In and out, y'know?"

Oh yeh, thought Joey, in and out; *I* know.

Defensive. "We were going to get photos and stuff and like memories and souvenirs, on the honeymoon. A swell honeymoon; swell memories; swell top-drawer stuff."

"You know," put in Joey, "this could be a tough case to crack. Guy could be on any one of seven or so continents, using who knows what name, hiding who knows where, and we don't even know what he looks like."

"You're the professionals; handle it," she snapped. "I gotta run."

"Yeh well, LaBelle — be seein'ya," I said.

But I was wrong.

Chapter Two

Willie's Wideworld Travel turned out to be a little second-floor walk-up over a pawnbroker's, next to a tattoo parlor, across from a pinky-nails place. One-stop shopping for all the stupidity of the world, in one tight place. It was just enough off the main routes of downtown that the rents start getting reasonable again. Not a lot of walk-in traffic, though. And those that might, mostly the kind, you'd just as soon they'd walk off somewhere else.

We figured we'd be milking this joint for all it was worth, since it was all we had to go on. Might want to try the innocent act twice, so Joey went on up alone while I stayed in the car. (Though, as things would turn out: Twice, but no dice. Snake eyes. Story of my life. Story of *this* case, in spades.)

He came back down in a couple of minutes and shrugged. Willie not there, apparently as per usual, bored black girl at the desk reading a magazine. Maybe LaBelle's permanent replacement, maybe just a temp; she hadn't inclined to autobiography. Had Joey's good friend Richie Mallow been in that afternoon? this Richie's good friend Joey inquired. —"No." Nobody had been in. Not: "Oh he left for Milan two weeks ago, sir, may I give you his hotel address?" And not: "He skipped out on his wife and won't be back." Or even: "What, do you mean the dealer in international Conflict Diamonds? No actually, he's dead; and his killer is right behind you, Luger in hand; he's been waiting for you to come in." None of that. Just: No.

After that, conversation lapsed a little; since in that situation, there is not much to talk about except sex and the weather: and anyone could plainly see it wasn't raining.

Then Joey tried again, Take Two, on a different tack: saying he had to find his good friend Richie who, he knew, flew, flew off two weeks ago, he thinks to Europe, he thinks ... ahh .... Richie mentioned something ... was it ...? ah, it's gone; and could she just please-as-a-favor to a friend-of-Richie's, just maybe quick check her files? — Now this actually did not tally real well, with Joey's supposedly coming in looking for him there, that very afternoon, his earlier story from just thirty-seven seconds ago; and this Sheila maybe sensed this. (Some babes are born yesterday; some ain't.) Anyhow she gave him the breeze.

LaBelle wasn't home so we checked out the business registry to find out Willie's last name: Harfrock. Home phone not listed. "Looks like a stakeout," I say to Joey, and he sighs. Stakeouts are not the most glamorous part of detective work — not a patch on high-speed car-chases and rooftop shoot-outs, which are the usual way I get my exercise — in fact it can be pretty humiliating, sitting there for hours and hours, in a car, with a jar ....

The travel girl's already seen Joey and dismissed his line of bull, so I go alone next morning at the crack of dawn — at our place dawn begins to crack its joints round about ten o'clock — with a supply of beverage and peanuts, and wait in the car with my hat pulled down and the collar pulled up, even though it's almost summer, across from the agency and a little ways down, with good sightlines on who goes in or out. Some guy looks like maybe an owner goes in and doesn't come out again in fifteen-twenty minutes, that'll be him.

I sit; I wait; I check the clock. Outside, no action. Time ticks by. And the warmth is getting to me, plus the soothing beer; and in time, perhaps I drift off just a little, catch forty winks — no, heck, no more'n twenty; but long enough to dream a little bit.

(I cross the street, walking through molasses. Facing the building like a mirror — a blind mirror with no image in it. I lift the plywood, fingers feeling its sweet real texture. And I am so glad to be here, feeling that sweet deep wood against my fingers, so glad I am almost weeping, as it — creaking, lifting — actually makes a moan.

Dark beyond it. Black, black; stark, dark. Go to it — Murphy or whatever your name is. That is the path that you have to travel. That is the row that you have to hoe.)

19

Three hours and the same number of peanut-bags later, he still has not showed, but I did learn one thing: that place doesn't get much customers. And Willie isn't there much, just like she says. Must have another job.

My good luck, there's a bar right across from the agency, with a big enough window to do my surveillance. I go in for a warm pee and a cold beer: my last cold bottle gave up the ghost in the car about the middle of the June morn. I sit at the end of the bar where I got a good look at the agency entrance. And sure enough, this guy goes in. But on the other hand, it's lunchtime, maybe he's one of the few guys left that actually work nine to five so's he can support all the other folks get their money from the government or just selling little scraps of paper back and forth. Working sucker on his lunch hour. And sure enough, he's back out in minutes with his ticket to Cleveland or wherever. So I put away a few more beers in the line of duty, and about two o'clock I start getting that feeling you get when your little body valves start crying out: Pizza, pizza! And the little mozzarella-receptors are all gone dry and standing there like orphans and the red tomato cells are all in an uproar, but I hang tough, I don't leave my post. So I chomp a few pretzels keep the beer busy and then wash them back with a few more beers because you'd be surprised how many guys buy the farm when one of them dry pretzel-sticks gets lodged sidewise in their gullets. Why just the other day—

Guy in a rumpled suit going up the stairs hasty, not like it's the first time he's been there. I check the time; and when I check it again, he been in there twenty minutes. Murphy makes his move.

Easier said than the other thing since all that beer there seems to of went straight to my feet; but I make it over somehow, and the fresh smog revives me and I straighten my T-shirt to a professional angle and head on up.

Same girl's there, or her twin sister, same broad and same bored. The guy I spotted earlier is in back with his feet up, reading a folder. The girl doesn't know me from Adam but at least I'm not Joey since the J-man sort of messed things up a little, contradiction-wise. I go up to the guy and enquire, "Are you Mr. Harfrock?" He looks up pretty sharply, like: How do I know his name. Good question, I should've thought something up in advance; just keep talking and maybe he won't think about it anymore either. "A good friend of mine bought a ticket here two weeks ago, forgot to leave his address where he'd be. His mother is awful sick, might not make it, wants to get in touch." I don't actually know if he bought a ticket here or if he bought one at all: but if he didn't then I got no leads whatever, so I might as well risk it.

He looks me over. "Real sick, eh?"

"Something awful."

"What she got?"

"Ahhhh, the epizooties, I think it was; with complications."

"Lot of that going around," he says sympathetically.

"Yeh," I say, "a girl can't be too careful."

He nods. "This friend of yours have a name?"

"Yeh! He got one of those. Name's Richie; and his last name, why, same as his dear old Ma's."

"And that would be?"

Truth-time. "Mallow. Richie Mallow."

He gives me a big smile — a little too big. "And you'd be wanting me to do what."

"Well I just thought you might maybe remember where the ticket was for, or else you might, um, check right there in those files right there," I say, pointing with a diffident finger at some cabinets right behind him. "Might even have the hotel he made the reservation at — maybe a phone number for contact — maybe a photo or an SSN number, credit cards — that kind of thing."

"It might at that."

Then a little time passes with him standing there smiling, rocking gently back and forth on his part-shiny, part-scuffed saddle shoes, and me standing here trying to work up an answering smile. Finally he says:

"You're no friend of Richie's. You got dick written all over your face."

I wipe it with my sleeve and then I realize he means *shamus*; and fact of the matter I'm real pleased. Most folks, they get a look at my mug and play What's My

Line, they size me up for something not that flattering; like: pickpocket, or crash-car dummy, or sideshow geek. So I figure I'll come clean with him — anyhow clean as I generally come.

"That's right," I say, "I'm a detective," and I hand him a phony card. He looks it over shaking his head, and I add: "In the interests of justice, do you think you could see your way clear to just checking those files?"

"What's he done?"

"Nothing I know of, he just disappeared. And there really is a dame worried about him, — his mom just got all better but now it's his wife."

He raises a part of an eyebrow like he didn't know the guy was married and didn't much envy whoever might have tied the knot with that guy. It's a cinch he doesn't know the bride is LaBelle or he'd ask how she was doing, chew over some old times, after all she'd worked for him a couple of months before she left.

But he says: "No dice."

I am getting very near the bottom of my bag of tricks. So I dump the rest out onto his desk. "The wife in question just happens to be one of your former employees."

The eyes narrow. "And that would be —"

"A Miss LaBelle — well you know, Mrs. now but she was Miss back then — a Miss LaBelle Le-"

He blows up at me then, face like a stroke and waving his dinky arms. "You can tell that little b —" and then he uses a word that he hadn't not oughta since another one is present. Guess that note she left on his monitor must've been pretty strong. But then he instantly dials it down and says, with a voice like ice: "You're a detective — so whyncha go *detect* something." A jerk of his head informs me of the general direction of the door.

So I shrug and head out and say, "If you change your mind, call me." I know he won't change his mind and anyhow if he does call the number on the card, all he'll get is a pizza to go.

I drive back to the fort and tell Joey the not-so-good news. "Forget Christmas dinner at the Harfrocks' this year. It's off."

He describes to me the girl now in more detail, and it sure sounds like the exact same girl. "And now she'll be speaking up saying that some guy was in just the day before asking the same questions," I moan.

"But we fooled 'em," observes Joey. "Different guys."

"Yeh so he'll say, Whadya mean, *some* guy — **same** guy? And she'll say No, though maybe a family resemblance, same type of T-shirt in fact, and he'll know that there's two of us working on the case. So now he knows more than *we* do, and I don't like those odds."

So we're both pretty glum and we go drown our sorrows in a large one with anchovies, only thing to cheer a guy up at a time like this.

Chapter Three

I called LaBelle's place several times before finding her in, and said we had no leads yet. She didn't seem too interested. I asked if Richie had left anything at her apartment — anything at all. I don't know what we would've done with it if he had — dusted for fingerprints? give it to a bloodhound? Anyhow he hadn't.

Conference with Joey. Two wise heads deep in thought. We chew the fat this and we chew the fat that, and finally I get an idea.

My pappy used to tell me — would have if he'd ever been at home — : Set a thief to catch a thief. So we decided to knock over Willie's files.

LaBelle had quit the firm, but maybe Richie had still used Willie's outfit for his tickets. *Probably*, even, since supposedly he knew Willie from outside work. It was worth a chance.

We got together our kit for people that forgot their keys, and headed downtown at around four of the a.m. Streets almost deserted; but then we spot a cop car. We wait at the curb for the thing to blow away like a bad smell. It moves on, we get out, we see *another* cop car heading in from the opposite direction. What gives? We feel a sudden urge to be back in the car driving away; and we satisfy this urge.

"What's up?" asks Joey.

"Must be the bank branch across the street. Another bank got knocked over yesterday, third this month. Looks like the coppers are patrolling the block."

"So what do we do?"

"We go back and we sleep. Then we get up and think this thing through."

The next morning bright and early, just shy of noon, we're enjoying a hearty breakfast of fried eggs on pop-tarts, and I have my big idea.

"We go in like Santa Claus. Climb up from the next street over, which is dead, then down the hatch."

"What hatch."

"We'll find one."

The buildings in the older part of downtown got so many setoffs and cornices and doodads and stuff, not to mention the fire escapes, a rock-climber type could sleepwalk up one; but me and Joey made it easy on ourselves and brought rope and a home-made grappling hook. It's just a two-storey building anyway, and we were up it before you could say James James Morrison Morrison Weatherby George Dupree.

We pried off a vent cover and went down the ventilation duct, through a crawl space, and then just kicked through the flimsy part of the ceiling between the beams. It was pretty neat, just us and a flashlight, like a haunted house. The file cabinets were unlocked and I started with the top one. Thumb thumb thumb thumb thumb. The detective, crafty at his craft.

Then I heard a thump and figured it was Joey but Joey knew it wasn't him. "There's someone downstairs," he said.

I can't believe the cops could've spotted us in the dark up on the roof the two seconds we were up there, plus the angle would have been bad from the prowl car, since we came from the rear. But Joey wanted to poke his head down the stairs, see what was up.

Silence.

"Looks like there's nobody here, Murph."

He goes a little further, just to make sure.

"All right *freeze*!" I hear a voice coming up the stairs. Joey, I reckon, freezes; he's pretty cool to begin with.

"Oh, plainclothes, is that it? Keep your hands up, copper, we're traveling. One peep or one hit of the beeper and you're a dead man."

We suddenly both realize what has happened. Some yegg's knocking over the pawnshop downstairs same time's we're partying upstairs. He thinks Joey's a cop but he doesn't want to kill him because (A) Murder One, and (B) the other cops, the real ones this time, the ones in uniform, would come running at the sound, so he figures all's he can do is to use him as a hostage or a human shield to make a getaway.

It's almost funny, really. Actually not even almost — Joey starts to grin and to chuckle and then he cracks up. And believe me, when that brother gets to laughing, his laughter fills the room. He's just rocking back and forth, shoulders helplessly heaving, wiping away tears. And the hard guy, he said he was gonna plug him if he tried to call his pals, but this laughing jag he hadn't figured on, it just doesn't add up — doesn't add, subtract, or multiply, or ... that other thing that he forgets, oh right, shoulda stayed in school. So he's fingering the trigger and the possibilities are whirling like the fruit in a slot machine that doesn't stop, and Joey's laughing and laughing, holding his sides, and the poor guy is just standing there not the least bit plussed. So I saunter down holding a tire-iron gunwise, and say, Drop it (in a sort of a cop accent, from the side of the mouth where the butt would go if you could smoke on duty), and he does. "You have the right to remain silent," I begin; but then it's just too funny — Joey explodes anew at my routine and soon I'm laughing too, each brother's reaction egging on the other, like a couple of maniacs.

The burglar turns out to be just a kid, practically, very nervous and green, with a gat but still green, and he does not know what thing is happening to him. He's heard of the good cop bad cop shtick, but the Two Loony Cops, each one loonier than the other, that number is new to him, and doesn't compute. He cannot handle it. I'm thinking about putting him up against the wall and tossing him as he might be carrying some tools that could might aid us in our work, but then I notice what a botched job he's made of the pawnshop door. He had managed to get past the outside front door, all right, you could open it with a stick of gum; but then in the tiny entryway there's a steel-grate-covered glass door to the pawnshop, next to the stairwell that leads up to the agency. He's been smashing the glass and made a mess and he's no closer to getting in than he was before. I shake my head. What is this country coming to, the youth, no pride in their work, the old craft traditions, I mean, tell me about it, gramps. And me, I got a soft heart. Say what you like, a soft head too maybe, but I just can't help taking pity on the kid.

"Here, look, whacha got here. ... Hm, not too s'phisticated; but it's a bad workman blames his tools, my pappy always would of said if he had said it. Let's see if we can work this thing in right here ... The-re ... Look sharp now, observe the elbow action, up and down, there she's coming, I tell ya, it's all in the wrist." The metal door swings open. As does the kid's mouth.

"What is this — entrapment?"

"Naw, it's a birthday present. For Piglet's birthday. Be my guest."

He looks now from one to the other. "You're not coppers?"

I lean into the light, and give him my leery grin.

"You're not coppers," he says, as the penny drops. And the fact is, nobody would ever mistake me for a copper if the light was right. Might mistake me for a side of beef, but copper I am not.

"We're from the Civil Liberties Union," I say. "Criminal Assistance Division. Help yourself."

He's freaked, he's shaking, maybe we scared him straight.

"Can — can I go now?"

"Sure, there's the door. That rectangley thing over there."

He splits into the night, hopefully to go join a monastery.

We go back up chuckling about how the pawnbroker will come in the next morning, find the glass all smashed up and the place broken into, but find nothing, not a thing gone. Might just get religion too.

"Hey," says Joey, "he just went out the *front*. What if the cops see him coming out and get suspicious?" That is a very intelligent remark.

"Shoot, we blew it. Okay, you scoot up the chute to the roof, scope the streets, and I'll take a look around upstairs real quick. Hold the rope loop down to pull me up pronto if you give me the whistle."

But no such bum luck — the kid had slipped out between prowl-car drive-bys, and I spent the next fifteen minutes unmolested, pawing through Willie's files. Nothing alphabetically at *Mallow*, nothing at *Richard* or *Richie* either. Nothing anywhere. Which maybe explains why the files were left unlocked — why risk me jimmying it. But actually this tells me something further. If Willie really was smart, he'd leave the file and just pull what was sensitive, like apparently the last ticket, which I don't know if he ever had a chance to draw it up. But I *know* that Mallow had a file, so this was clumsy.

I learn another thing. Here in the customer list is one Franco Romano — a fellow also known as Hawkeye. Never met him, but I know him by rep. Bad company. But still, that doesn't mean that *this* company is bad, Willie's little shoestring agency, or that Mallow is necessarily bad just because he's on Willie's list along with a bad customer. Guy's gotta fly, gotta buy cigarettes. Gotta do business *somewhere.* Doesn't mean that the place he picks his smokes is a front for the mob. Still, it's a nice little factoid to know, even if it doesn't connect to anything yet. Especially since it is practically the only thing I do know in the whole case.

We get home at last, tired and happy, celebrate the night's triumphs, and sleep the sleep of the drunk.

The next day, in the cold grey dawn of noon when we get up, we don't feel so good. It was fun at the time, but when you look at it point-blank, in that un-drunk cold light, we basically come up with point-nothing. We don't even know for certain that Willie's got anything to hide. I'd been spinning all these neat plots in my head, there in the dark with the flashlight, but maybe it's something simple. Maybe Willie just don't like mugs coming in taking files of his customers. Heck, *I* wouldn't. Or maybe he just took out Mallow's file and was looking it over at home for some reason, going over golden memories, playing Travel-Agent Trivia. Who knows. So we maybe, *maybe*, got one small piece, but we got no jigsaw puzzle. So nothing fits.

So I sit around reading *Ellery Queen*, and Joey goes out to his friend Sammy's and we just let the afternoon truck on by at its own pace. Around four o'clock, Joey comes back, big smiles, says he won a bundle on the gerbil races and we can go get the TV out of hock. "Great," I say, "let's can this case and just watch TV."

So we call up Miss-or-Missus Le-Baron to give her the bad news, but she doesn't pick up. We let it ride. We call an hour later and she's not there. We have a beer. (A beer each, natch; it's not like me and Joey ever split beers, that would be like what Solomon was gonna do to that baby.) We call again, ditto, so Joey says let's just go over there and leave a note. Then we can wash our hands of this thing. Tell her we're pulling off pronto unless she can come up (A) with some cash, or (B) with some clues; or any combination of the above.

She's got an apartment in one of these security buildings, they're supposed to buzz you in. There are ways around that, though. Anyhow we buzz her, she's maybe in the shower, we walk around the block and take in the sights and buzz her again. Still no answer. So we walk around the block again only this time in the other direction, clockwise, case we missed any subtleties in the scenic landscape the first time. And in fact, this time around, the dumpster looks especially picturesque, seen from a different angle in a different light. We buzz again, she's not in. I figure I'll just leave her a note, but all we have to write on is this piece of pizza box, and these tiny mailboxes, they just got these little mean slits, I mean it's worse than a Presbyterian virgin, the message won't fit. And I want to make sure that she gets her message, so we let ourselves in another way, without a key, and tromp on up the stairs — no elevator — to her apartment on the next-to-top floor. First I knock, just in case she's back and the buzzer isn't working inside; then I rap out *shave-and-a-haircut* a few times because it's fun to do and because, even if she's in there having a shower or making love or pulling a Greta Garbo, *nobody* can resist eventually knocking back answering, *two bits*. So I'm scribbling out the message on the bit of box, and Joey kneels to shove it under the door, and then says, Hey, Murphy, get a load of this. Blood.

No, not running out in floods from under the door, like a movie, just a print on the bare floor between the door and the runner, just one thin crescent, like a heel left it. Not even really red now, more like brown, but you get so you recognize these things.

I try the door; it's locked. She got a police lock and that would take some doing but I give it the old shoulder try anyway and it gives. The police lock wasn't

33

on. There was just the little nothing lock you get when you push the little button on the doorknob on your way out. The police lock needs a special key, and whoever pushed that button on his way out either didn't have the key or was in a hurry.

We close the door behind us and walk in slowly, really taking our time. It's not like there was anyone lying in wait for us; and if there was, he already heard us when we shoved in the door, so we needn't be quiet, but we do get quiet nonetheless, stock-still and real quiet, listening to the way the silences are softly bouncing off the walls. It's how a blind guy finds his way around. So I listen and I sniff, not a creature is stirring. But there is death in the air and I can almost smell it, almost hear its faint and fading dying sigh.

The body is in the bedroom. Professionally done. Not much blood, a single small-caliber bullet in exactly the right place, either she was sleeping and the guy could take his time and come up close, or else he's very, very good.

I'm betting he is very, very good. (The little hairs stand up on the back of my neck, where the bullet would go.)

But something made him go back later into the bedroom, after the wound had had time to bleed. He didn't find what he was looking for in the entry room, and went back in; and that is when he got a little on his heel. So whatever he was looking for, he probably didn't get; but she got it in the neck, just the same.

We search through it all ourselves, just going through the motions. It's kind of discouraging, since we have almost no hope of finding whatever it was the killer wanted to find, unless he had to leave in a hurry, and it doesn't look that way. Things are a little bit disturbed but not just thrown about. Picture frames hanging a little crooked, stuff like that. Heck, this place looks neater *after* it has been tossed, than my place looks ever. So again, a professional. All we get to see is what he didn't bother to take.

There is no money anywhere, not a dime. Now, the stuff you read about in books, seven hundred dollars left in a drawer and the thing that's missing turns out to be the Secret Plans, that's baloney. Ninety-nine guys out of a hundred will take cash if it's lying around in mixed bills. Even if they don't need it — even if they got millions, even if they're rich as Jesus, or however the saying goes — why would you *not* take it? So you can tip off the cops that it wasn't a simple burglary? So the case can be handed to the smart guys at the FBI instead of the local snatch squad, who never recover anything anyway and are barely expected to? No, you got any brains, you go ahead and take the cash, even if it's only icing on the cake, even if you flush it down the toilet after you take the cake. In fact, for all we know it *was* the cake.

Only I don't think so. First, the building's not that fancy, plus you had to work your way around that police lock; burglars prefer low-hanging fruit. Next, the killing is too clean. Say you're knocking over an apartment, owner walks in on you, okay, you got a problem and maybe instead of just skipping out, you handle it in a rough way, which you will probably later regret, because now you've got Homicide after your ass whereas, other way, it's an attempted burglary where nothing got actually burgled; very low-pri — hand it to your least-brightest guy. Now, a guy might panic, there's a body but it's still basically a burglary; only, this thing is way too expert and way too pre-meditated. He gets past the police lock so smooth he doesn't even wake her, or rouse her from putting on make-up at the mirror, then creeps up and a single shot to the back of the neck; and then this careful, unrushed, putting-things-nicely-back-afterwards search-through. Heck, you're as good as that, you make way more from a contract killing than from everything that was in the apartment, including the ten-cent-off coupons and the S&H Green Stamps. No, he was looking for something. Or else, he *wasn't* looking for something and it was a plain contract killing but he made it *look* like he was looking for something, just to drive Murphy crazy. Which he succeeded and did.

Joey comes in from the bathroom where he's been rummaging around. "Hey, Murphy, lookit this. She got some kina laser weapon, or I don't know what. Only ya gotta plug it in. Darnedest thing I ever seen."

"Stow that, Joey, just some contraption for gals. Dames use it to dry their heads."

Joey, with his Butch cut, turns it this way and that, uncertainly. Why would you want to dry your *head*?

I go back to going through the drawers. Joey gives up and goes back into the john.

Clothes and stuff, but nothing that tells me anything. No merry widows or crotchless panties, no tickets to East Berlin taped to the underside of a drawer, no map of tunnels hidden behind a mirror, and nothing that Mallow might've left behind. Definitely all dame stuff.

"Hey Murphy buddy, lookit. She got this little tiny soft-rubber Frisbee or something. Like for playing Frisbee with a hamster." He opens its powder-blue case.

"Joey, just leave it alone, willya? Help me look for clues."

Joey looks put out. "So what do *clues* look like, Murphy?"

Good question. "They come with little clue-tags on 'em, whadoo I know? Like, 'Hello, I'm Clue #2.'" Joey's even more put out and I apologize. "Sorry, Joey, *I* don't know. Just anything that tells us what her game was. Which we probably already know: game of gold-digger. Heck — not even that — just a regular jane, got a regular job, bumps into some gold a guy dumps in her lap. Fool's gold. She may be a fool, but she isn't — wasn't — a villain."

37

Joey takes this in and seems to agree, but then he sits down in a chair and sort of tunes out. I wonder, as I go back to hit the closets, why I am even doing this, why I don't just chuck it too, now that our (anyway-unpaying) client is dead.

Well I'll tell you why. Because there's nothing the heck good on TV.

The next hour drags. Joey's wishing he'd brought a comic book. The apartment is not exactly furnished like a waiting room — no toys or teddies for the kids, and no decent magazines, not even an old *Readers Digest* or *National Geographic*, just a couple of monthlies that they're about hair. I mean, can you figure that? *Hair*? A whole magazine, just about *hair*? Like, *Quarterly Review of Toenails* or *International Journal of Elbows*. Hair!

Dames.

And then I find something. Not something cleverly hidden cause then the other guy would've found it. Something obvious and not obvious. The municipal phone book, lying out in plain view.

Not her personal address book, either she didn't have any or the guy took it. Just the plain old clunky-chunky phone book same as everybody has.

But consider the lady, and consider the scene. No books, no desk, no notepads, no pens, and just a single stubby pencil in the whole place. This is not your basic

Renaissance scriptorium. She led a life of hair, of gabble gabble gabble, no need to write anything down. Unless, of course, one day someone called you at home with something very important and unexpected. Quick, what to do? Me I understand perfectly; I just wrote my own resignation note on a piece of pizza box. The only thing to write on is the phonebook, lying right next to the phone. And the only thing to write with — remember now, she's a dame — is lipstick, one of over a dozen different sticks in various shades by my count, at least one of which is never out of arm-reach, no matter where she might be in the room. (Never know when you might need a New You.) So we leaf through it and, pretty soon, bang, the red leaps out — actually kind of a funky off-red, you can be sure they got a name for it, dames, "torrid peach" maybe — where she has written in lipstick, in a blank margin in the yellow pages next to an ad for intercity buses:

fri 2 pm lido pink scabroso

I stare at this a long time. A message from the grave.

Joey looks and whistles. "Bingo!"

"Well no, bingo is when all your numbers line up right down the line. This is just something to go on."

I look sadly back at the client now, that wrote that, a person we never really knew and now never will. Too late for last rites. Too late for sorry, too late for good-bye. Well, rest her soul — whoever you are, and wherever that soul may be.

Joey feels sad too, and also troubled. "You think we oughta call the cops?"

"Call the what? Joey you feelin' okay?"

"Just seems like she oughta get buried."

"Oh, they'll find her soon enough. We'll call up the super, anonymous, complain about the loud radio in 33B. — Oh hey though, good thing you mentioned it. Don't want the bulls to be too far ahead of us in this game."

I rip out the page with the message from the phone book, along with a bunch of others. Then I write "Hawke" on another scrap of pizza box, right up to where it's torn, and place the fragment in her hand. Then I take the lipstick and write on the mirror:

DEATH TO WHOEVER QUESTIONS OUR MASTER, NOSTRADAMUS

Then I put the little crucifix, what she had on her wall in the john, upside-down in front of an ashtray, like it was a little altar to the guy with horns.

"That'll give'em something to chew on."

We go home and I'm kind of brooding about it all. Joey goes off to Sammy's, and two hours later he comes back brooding too. Backed a bum gerbil and blew his whole wad. Bye-bye Perry Mason; hello square one.

Dinner that night comes down to home-made pizza pop-tarts. Same as your basic individualized pizzas, only for crust you use a pop-tart. Melt on one of those good American cheese squares, add ketchup, and vwala: pizza à la Murphy.

We'd rather send out for a large, the kind that tastes good, but the jack has gotten scanty again, and beggars got no choice at all, as my pappy used to say (though not within my earshot).

The conversation is not exactly thriving as we sit around the kitchen table munching cold pop-tarts (toaster's in hock); plus what, the radio's broke.

We chew and think and avoid each other's gaze. I know what's on his mind, he knows what's on mine. And neither the one of us is real eager to bring it up.

Finally Joey pops the question.

"So *now* whadawe do?"

I shrug. "I figure we just keep on looking for him."

"Yeh but now nobody's hiring us."

"So what, she wasn't paying us anyway."

"Just seems weird."

"It's either that or just watch TV."

"TV's in hock."

"Well then that settles it."

Another thing. It's bothering me how I mentioned LaBelle to Willie in connection with Mallow, and then she turns up dead. Coincidence? Not that I think Willie did it or even had it done. He was p'd off, sure, but he wouldn't have her zeroed just for that. And even if he'd wished he could, he wouldn't want to fork out the five thou, ten thou smackers it must've took to have the job done right, like it *was* done. To do a thing like that, he'd have to have a much bigger reason than that she just quit on him, nasty note or no nasty note. And if he did have any connection with the hit, then why would he cuss her out like he did, right in front of the detective? No, Willie's out; but he might've maybe mentioned it to someone, who passed it on to a party, who told it to a guy — either about Richie getting hitched, or about two gumshoes coming around looking for him — on *her* orders, near as he could tell. So it wasn't about her; it was about Richie. Which makes him more interesting, as a quarry. Wish we had some clues, though. Cases are supposed to come with clues.

We polish off the tarts and dig in to a hearty dessert of chocolate syrup. Joey's poured his into a beer-mug, me I'm licking the good stuff right of the lid of the can.

Joey says wisely, "You better watch out wit'at, get a rusty cut, they gotta pucha on anabotics, cost a buncha dough."

I nod and say nothing. Joey's mixing his with beer, got a kind of soda float going.

"Wonder what's on TV tonight," I say, looking out the window. "Out there."

Joey looks out too. He can tell I'm getting depressed

"He-ey, brother," says Joey gently. "Hey, man, 'smatta witchoo. You ever listen to the tee-vee with the sound off?"

"Yeh, lots of times, it's real restful."

"Yeh well then, so it's even more restful with the picture off, too."

Good old Joey. We both watch the dark through the window-frame, like a ghost TV set, and watch the snowflakes slowly falling in our imagination.

That night I consult my pillow, but the pillow clams up, and when we get up in the morning, I got no new ideas. So we roll with the punches and go move the moose head off the pool table to play a game. I get some of my best ideas playing pool. Only mostly they're about pool.

Pock pock, ina pocket. Eight-ball don't darken my door.

We don't talk much; we let the balls do the talking. But today I am off my game.

"Hey Murphy," pipes up Joey. "I gotta question."

"Question, huh? Something you were wantina ask me?"

"Yeh, sump'm along those lines."

"Okay, shoot."

"The thing is — how're we ever gonna find Mallow when we don't know where he was going, let alone where he is by now, not even what ocean is closest, or what he looks like, or what his game is, or what kinda rare Tibetan tobacco he smokes so we can say Aha! when we come across some? Plus we got no money for expenses, no money period. And our track record, well ... the most we ever find in our life what was lost, is just *car* keys: and they were for a different car."

I nod. Good question. A three-Camel problem. I nod again.

Just tryina line up this shot ....

Pock! Plunk. Got it.

I straighten up.

"Y'know, Joey, you got a good idea there with those keys. Like they say, the drunk guy looking for his keys beneath the lamppost, not because he lost them there but because that's where there's light; and everybody laughs. But what they don't realize is that the drunk was *right*. He's got no idea where he dropped his keys, they could be anyplace out in acres and acres of dark; but he's got this one good spot where he can see everything, find something useful, maybe not his keys but maybe a lock-pick. All kinds of things would do."

"Yeh," Joey rubs his chin, "I remember that parable from the Bible. I think. Only, how does that help us out?"

"We'll see —" and I hunch over and I warm up to it and I'm getting into it again, Murphy on a winning streak, the Murph-man on a roll. "Face it — Mallow is to heck and gone, far as we know: out in those acres of dark. But now we got the LaBelle Murder Case right here in our own little circle of light — and it ties into Mallow somehow. It's a real case — and a case where we got clues! So let's use 'em! Think I'll call it — *The Case of the Dead Ditched Dame*."

Joey's eyes are glowing now; we're back in business.

"See, ya gotta go at it like Napoleon woulda done — no, you wouldn't know 'im, French guy, short guy — or like Knute Rockne. Ya gotta have a strategy — a plan."

Joey vigorously nods agreement.

"And see, my plan is, why not — you know, the guy that iced her? — we ask him, *Whyja do it*? It probably ties in."

Joey's eyebrows gather. "You sure are the idea man, Murph. Only ... no I *don't* know. Who's the guy?"

"Well see, that's the *next* part of my plan. We *find out*. — We're detectives, remember?"

Joey brightens. "Right! We find 'im, then we ask 'im." Then he darkens. "What if he won't talk?"

"You kidding? Give him one of your nice smiles, he'll pour his heart out."

Now, Joey weighs in on the far side of two hundred pounds, mostly muscle. And we were too poor to afford the tooth fairy when we were kids, so he's only got like a tooth here, a tooth there; and when he gets one of his grins going, well, if you don't know where he's coming from, that he's mostly really gentle, it can be hard to control your bowels.

"Yeh," says Joey. "Plus we can offer him part of our pizza. He'll be so glad. — Only, how do we get in touch with this guy?"

"Same way *anybody* hires himself a hit man. Just put out the word."

What it is — Me and Joey live kind of on the fringe, and most of the guys we know are even fringier, and some of them got friends like you wouldn't want them for baby sitters. So we let the word go out and the buzz go round that a certain party unnamed wants a certain citizen greased and is willing to pay for it, no questions asked. A party that wants quality and pays cash.

Lessen a day, this mug shows up for a job interview. All dressed up for it — black shirt, black tie, the works; must've been the teacher's pet in Gangster School. Turns out he mostly does kneecaps but for a price he'll stretch a point. We turn him down, but tell him he'll get a commission if he can come up fast with a guy who can do a clean hit and a discrete crib job at the same time. For that, you need a specialist. A B and E, fine; a hit, okay, but you want to hit and run. Hit and stick around, it's harder than the sum of the parts. Costs more; and we mention a figure about a thousand dollars higher than even what you might expect. With an extra bonus if it's done today.

"This is really neat," says Joey, admiring my clever plan. "We just sit in a pizza booth and the fish comes to us."

"Yeh, only this one's a barracuda. Try not to taste too much like a worm, okay, Joey?"

We're not generally known for hiring this kind of thing but it's a big town, people from nowhere blow in all the time. And one look at us, one smell, tells you we're not cops. You might guess pimps, pimps for legless prostitutes; or a moochie that goes around a TB clinic stealing barf bags; but not cops.

If the guy we're looking for's a freelance, which they mostly are in that racket, chances are he'll come around, at least to check us out. The cash is not bad, but more than that, he'll want to know who the players are, case he crosses their paths again. And if the guy's on contract to an organization — sort of a house hit-man — and doesn't take other work, he'll still want to come around and see who's the new boy in town that's outbidding his boss. Either way we get somebody to share the pizza and talk about old times.

We are just about to order another round when a man walks in and, without asking, joins us at our corner booth, just past the door that leads to the john, where we are out of earshot. He is thin, pale, featureless, medium height. He does not look as though he weeps at movies.

"Make it three?" I ask, gesturing with a glass.

47

He shakes his head, just a slight little shake. "Don't order anything."

"Suit yourself," and I hold up two fingers.

What he says next is not literally loud but he has selected a harder grade of metal and it slices into me like a meat cleaver. "I said: Don't order anything. Not for me, not for you."

My arm wilts. Joey frowns: a bad sign.

Lips almost not moving; the eyes — on mine — definitely not. "Describe the job."

This could be our man, all right. I skip the introductory pleasantries. "A party of the feminine gender has certain private correspondence which my employer wants returned to their rightful owner, namely, him. They are almost certainly hidden in her apartment, though we don't know exactly where. They are probably bound with blue ribbon, possibly not, but they are all addressed to Miss Susan R. Darlin, just exactly like that, in plain business envelopes with no return address. These will be the letters, you do not need to open the envelopes. As for Miss Darlin, she must cease to exist, cease without a sound; and her mortal remains are to be found in her apartment, but not right away. Make it look like a regular robbery. Everything very quiet, very hushed."

If you had a magnifying glass you might've seen him nod. He looks at me for what feels like a long time after I have said my piece; I'm wishing I'd been able to order that other beer so that I'd have a place to hide the expressions on my face. Finally he says, "I can handle that."

"It's not that easy. You'll have to track her movements, find out when she is certain to be home. And it's a security apartment."

He purses his lips a little like why am I insulting him with these schoolboy details.

"And one other thing: She's got a police lock. But you can't go in like gangbusters — no noise. The walls are thin; one scream, one phone call and you're finished. And I mean literally. My employer does not wish to be connected with any unpleasantness in any way; a couple of his representatives will be observing the proceedings from a secure location, ensuring silence if silence is required."

This doesn't seem to bother him. "Sounds interesting. Cost extra."

"Extra's no problem."

"Two thirds in advance."

I hesitate a moment to show I'm leery of this departure from the normal fifty-per-cent up front; then I say, "That isn't a problem."

"Small bills."

And now it's my turn to pretend to be insulted. I scoff, "Of course small bills. What you think he's gonna write a personal check? — So okay, you've named your conditions, here's ours. You slip up in any way, you tip your hand, she'll scram, and sell the letters to someone else. Fatal for all concerned. So how do we know you

can handle it?" Go for the pride. "You got —
references?" A grin.

Still no emotion. "I can handle it. And references?
Yes. Just ask around. Nico offers quality to the
discerning customer. And I am Nico."

I hand Joey a skeptical glance and he hands it back
to me intact. "I'm sure you can hit a scampering
squirrel at fifty paces, but there is more to it than that.
You need to have the nerve to stick around and search
methodically, even while the corpse that could hang
you is lying on the floor."

A shrug — but now of annoyance; and with that
frail small human emotion, *pride*, he lets down his
guard. "I can *handle* it. I *have* handled it." Bingo. His
fatal mistake.

Okay, go for broke. "You as good as the guy what
did LeBaron?"

That was unexpected, and as swift as a kick to the
privates. And as cool as he is, he can't repress a flicker
in a couple of tell-tale muscles around the mouth.
Which means he has heard of the hit. Which is
interesting because it hasn't been reported yet. Of
course, that doesn't explain how *I've* heard of it, and he
drills in.

"Never heard of her. And how come *you* have."

"It was on the police scanner." Which it may well
have been.

He nods, tight-lipped, no way to call me on that
now. His mind briefly returns to its corner to consult

with the coach. Okay no problem. He can dig out the details later.

"I don't know anything about that," he lies. "But I can handle a scenario such as you describe."

Joey and I exchange consultative glances as though silently calculating the odds. Finally I say: "We'll have to chance it. Head over to Mama Tina's in one hour and we'll meet you with the two-thirds in cash."

"You will not," he says. This guy makes a cucumber feel like a hot tamale. "Neither of you gentlemen is leaving my sight. You gotta pee, we all go in together, just like the ladies. We all go together and get the money, right now, like three pals." He doesn't even bother to raise his voice — or lower it, for that matter — or pat his shoulder holster or shake his cuff where he hides his knife.

I shrug. "Okay by me."

I tell him we have it stashed at a certain deserted warehouse. We drive all in one car, that we borrow from where its owner apparently abandoned it for an hour or so, to the warehouse, that's not near anything but more urban desert. One of my favorite spots for family picnics.

He gets out, looks around, holds his hand up for silence, listens intently; and then, apparently satisfied, motions us in.

We're walking in, me first, then Nico, then Joey, when in a flash I swing around with a haymaker to the breadbasket. He doubles up; and before he can go for his tools of the trade, Joey slips on the cuffs.

He recovers quickly, and looks from the one to the other of us which what would probably have been a sneer if he ever bothered to register emotions on his face. "I do, not, believe this. If the cops are down to using mugs like you, they must be desperate. As a taxpayer, I'm incensed."

"Cops my buttress," I shoot back. "We're hit men, just like you."

A little puff of air, this guy's version of mirth. "Y ... *you*?" Like, What is this profession coming to, if he believed me, but he does not.

"That's right, I'm a hit man. You don't believe me?" So I hit him again.

The Murphy Might could maybe use a few more chin-ups and a few less beers. I didn't have the benefit of surprise this time, and he sort of dodged and feinted, even though cuffed, taking the sting out of the blow. He still didn't believe me.

Then Joey hit him.

When he woke up, he believed.

"Okay," he said, when he could talk again. "You've had your fun. What's your beef with *me*."

"We had a contract on the LeBaron dame. Supposed to deliver her *alive*. Then you barge in and ruin everything!"

This sets him back a bit. Just because he doesn't think we're anywhere near his class, doesn't mean that some rich party mightn't have hired us. "*You* had a contract? From who!"

"How do I know, this guy in a limo, and that's just the intermediary."

"Yeh well, whoever; but my assignment came straight from the Top; and whoever your guys might be, if they were interested in getting at a certain party through that LeBaron, they were either *working for* my guys, or they are probably already dead."

"Matter of fact, that might explain why they didn't answer, last time I called."

Of course I'm totally winging it; but you know that party game, you go around the circle, each person supplies a line, and before you know it, a semi-coherent story is building up. All I'm doing is flinging jigsaw pieces at him, that link up to some side of some piece that he throws out — there's no actual overall puzzle so far, but the pieces do seem to link, and it has got him off-balance.

"Could be; and if you don't want to join them in their coffin, you'll cut me loose right now. I already missed my call-in; my guys will be here soon."

This puts me into a musing mood. Might be straight-up; could be a ruse. But cutting him loose is a loser flat-out. So again, I mess with him a little. "You seem pretty confident in 'your guys'. But my guys ain't exactly stupid. Who are you trying to scare me with?"

He doesn't fall for that. "You wish. I'm not talking. Just wait and see."

I've only got one hole-card, and I play it now.

"Name 'Lido' mean anything to you?"

He is blank. It does not.

I make a stab at sarcasm. "Oh, so then it's Scabroso's outfit, you probably want me to believe."

And this time — he's good, but not so good that when you slam his mental solar plexus that he doesn't react just a ti-ny bit. That little flicker of the left eyebrow gave him away.

"Y'know," I add casually. "That's an interesting bunch, that is. Been thinking about hooking up with'em for some time. This town's gotten too small — nothing much going on."

His renewed look of contempt is starting to get to me. What, like I'm too dumb to work for your bunch? — Looking back on it, I shouldn't've let it get to me. Helped push me over the line.

I take Joey by the arm, leaving our friend with his arms in back, looped up over a standpipe. "Be right back. Sit tight, don't go 'way, 'K?"

When we're out in the lot behind the building, I breathe out. "Joey ... I'm not gonna enjoy this, and you, you sure as heck are not. But we got a guy in there that just does not, does not deserve the little fur-lined kid gloves. If we iced him right now, we'd be doing the world a favor — and him too, you come down to it, he'd have that much less later to answer for."

Joey has a look of horror. "You can't do that, Murphy, the guy is probably in a state of sin!"

"Yeh well, he don't look like he just come from Communion. But I ain't really talking about that. I want a bedtime story out of that guy — something to help me sleep at night. And he's going to need some persuasive encouragement."

"He-ey, Murphy, hey, lissena yourself, take it easy. We may be rogues, but we're not thugs."

"I know *you're* not, Joey; most days I'm not either. But this guy, that iced her, that's iced — who knows who-all, and he'll go on doing it. It's his job; maybe also his hobby."

Joey thinks hard. "Okay we ... we could uh, threaten to turn him over to the police."

This is the point where, in cartoonland, the listener's feet shoot out in front of him, a small shadow appears beneath to show that he's airborne, and exclamation points start popping out of his head, like ... like ... (help me out here)* [* "Like quills upon the fretful porpentine. "— Bard. — Eds.]

"O Ho *Ho*, said Santa Claus. Yeh that'll really shake him up. He probably already has a reserved cell downtown, complete with sauna and wet-bar. Cops are practically like headwaiters up there these days, bowing to a big-tipping guest. 'May we show you to your rights, sir? Oh no-no-no-no, please do not trouble yourself to say anything that might, *you* know, be used (perish the thought) against you (not that you have anything to hide), on the off-chance that this absurd little episode should ever make it as far as coming to trial. Which we assure you, sir, it will not. — Bed comfortable? Coffee warm enough? What — you only wanted *one* lump, and we gave you *two*?!? — Hey, O'Hara, let this guy go, we just violated his rights. — Please don't sue, sir. Have a nice day.' Any other suggestions?"

Joey looks miserable. He shook his head. I go on.

"I read somewhere in the Bible, where it says: If your right hand offends you, lop it off. Now, I don't know how Nico feels about it, but *his* right hand with that itchy trigger finger offends *me* right down to my drawers."

Joey nods; but says: "I can't do it, Murphy."

"I didn't think so, Joey. But I reckon I can."

Sad shake of the head. "Can't let you, there, Murphy. It's ... against the Law."

I have to laugh. "When did that ever stop us?"

And now he's waving his arms, there are maybe some tears there scratching to get out. "I don't mean Article 43-A, Murphy! I mean, God's law! Doesn't it say somewhere, No Rough Stuff — an amendment to the Ten Commandments maybe? What if it's a *sin*?"

The brother has a point there. I ponder this awhile, and then find myself saying: "I'll go to Confession."

Joey stares at me and his eyes pop out on stalks. "*You*? ... When was the last time you went to Confession?"

"Oh, now, hey, no need to take that tone, there, Joey. It's *been* awhile, been awhile; let's just say it's ... been awhile."

"Since you was a kid?"

"Oh hey don't rub it, don't grind it in. Let your brother alone."

"Murph I — you — I don't believe this. You would really do that? Really go?"

"I'd really do it."

"Honest Injun?"

"Scout's honor, Joey; and you know what *that* means."

He lets out a whistle and takes this in. *Scout's ... honor*! Him and me we never got to actually join the Scouts, but we really wanted to, we wanted to so bad ... It wasn't just they did cool stuff with knots; they had *honor* ... something we ourselves had never known.

I hear some roaring and rattling from inside where Nico is still chained to the pipe, but Joey doesn't notice.

"... Y'know ... ya gotta tell everything: ev-er-y-thing, since the last Confession. You can't just pick and choose."

The blood shoots into my ears. "What — even the *embarrassing* stuff?"

"'Fraid so, Murphy. It's worse than a prize fight. You'll come out pretty bloodied up."

I'm in over my head. Not the first time. "Okay okay. O-*kay*. Okay. Everything. Everything I can remember, anyhow. They must get cases like this, a guy can't specifically remember everything. I'll just give it to 'em bulk rate."

Joey's looking at me, uncomfortably like the collar-guy behind the grill. "Oh, you'll remember, Murphy. You're remembering right now."

The face is like a griddle now. "Gwan get outa here! I'm not remembering *that*!"

He lets it pass; sort of musing. "I mean, just take the *gluttony*, Murphy; least of the bunch, but just take that. Dijoo know gluttony was a sin? Uh-huh yep. Actually one of the Deadlies."

"Oh well hey, whaddya whaddya, like take like those pop-tarts, you know: they're really thin. Hardly any *meat* on 'em."

"Yeh but — the way you stack 'em, ten, twelve to a stack, with that Reddi-whip layered in between."

"Yeh well, a man's got an appetite. I don't eat past appetite. That's not gluttony, is it?"

"An'en when you just put your lips to the nozzle of the Reddi-whip can, and just — squee-eeeeeze ... O-oh, Murphy; and you don't stop till it's empty and you're full."

"Yeh well okay, point taken, might mention that. Note to self: Reddi-whip, my bad."

"An'a maple *syrup*, Murphy, the things you do with it, things God never intended them when he invented the little maple trees."

"What's with the — you tellin' me that stuff comes outa *maple* trees? Why would it do that? Tell it to the Marines!"

"Yeh, it does too, that's why they put it in those little log cabins, things. S'poseta remineja of trees."

"Aw you're making that up." More banging from inside; we ignore it. "Just reminds me of pancakes, Joey."

"Might be alright if ya just had the stuff on toppa pancakes, like regular Americans, it woulden be so bad. What if there's some angel guy, peepin' in the window, marking all this stuff down? But I mean the way you — *bob* ... for Tootsie Rolls, that're just swimmin' in it, o-oh Murphy, I just don't know."

"Okay me neither, but listen up. That guy's in there is waiting for me." A louder bang emphasizes the truth of this. "And I done all that stuff that I done, and I'm gonna tell the Father all about it; but right now I'm gonna do *one more thing*." And I head for the warehouse.

Joey calls after me. "I'll be out here prayin' for ya, Murphy."

I stop. I look back. "Thanks, Joey."

Our friend has not been idle. He's managed to drag a crate over with his toe and now he's standing on it and bent over forward and he's working the cuffs up towards the top of the pipe. Just a few inches from freedom.

"Siddown," I say, and I kick out the crate.

He comes down with a thunk. Doesn't bother him. "I don't have to talk to you."

I shake my head, slowly, sadly at his plight. "We're not cops, remember. We're hit men. And we're way behind in our reading of the Supreme Court rulings. So you do gotta talk. I'm dead afraid that you do."

He looks at me hard and steely. "You don't know who you're messing with, moron."

I lift his chin up with my curled finger. "But I do know. And that's *why* I'm messing with you."

I go back around and inspect his right hand like I'm thinking of buying it. "Is this the hand ya jerk off with? Oh — and is this your trigger finger, this little thing right there? Bad hand. It's gotta be spanked."

The guy's in a rage now, kept his cool for so long and now he's losing it — hurling it away, he's jerking forwards, practically ripping out the pipe.

"You can forget yer fun and games, idiot. *I don't got pain receptors! I just got hate receptors!* You better figure out quick how to kill me before my guys get here, 'cause I will hunt - you - down, you and your dumb brother, you and any worthless piece-of-shit friends and stupid relatives you may have."

It was maybe almost true. A guy in his line of work, he's got almost like this personal internal stash of morphine, dulls him to what he does — and dulls what others do to him. And I have to hand it to him, he did not once cry out over the next half hour while I was altering his hand. Only when the turn came around to his trigger finger, which I had carefully left till last, did it finally get to him. That was his livelihood, right there, in that one finger. And that livelihood was what he was all about — it was who he was and all he was. So he makes a calculation, then says, not like he's surrendering but like he just now thought of an angle:

"Actually, I know one or two things that might interest you."

I pour him a nip from my hip-flask. "I'd love to hear it." I sit down on the crate, all gathered round for story-time. "Oh and — sorry about the hand."

In the end we wound up giving him to the coppers anyway, for lack of any decent alternative. We tied him up, taped his mouth, and dumped him a little ways from the station, then called in anonymous with enough details out of what he told us to pin the LeBaron thing on him pretty clear and at least make them hold him for a day or so. He'd walk, of course, probably wouldn't even be charged; but the cops would be fretting, knowing they had the guy that done it even though they can't use my tips in court, and they'd be breathing down his neck for a few days, give us room and time to operate. And if they did charge him, and the court released him on his own recognizance or for a bail of ten gum wrappers or whatever murder goes for these days, he'd be wanting to skip town. The guy did have friends, but it turned out he was basically freelance, and the chances are he had just as many enemies as friends. We just might get away with it.

But Joey hadn't forgotten my promise, and now it was my turn. I picked a Catholic church out of the phone book. I even bought a new t-shirt, looked really nice. I said bye to Joey, all jaunty — then walked to the church like I was mounting a scaffold.

That Confession was just about the hardest thing I ever done. I've been on the wrong end of a P.D. third-degree in the good old days before all the rulings came down; I've had disagreements in alleyways, and played pool with poor losers, and even felt the wrath of a woman scorned. But what went on in that box, I come out dripping, staggering from side to side.

The Father in there must've felt at first a little out of his depth, like some truck just drove up and dumped a heap of garbage on his front lawn. But he warmed up pretty good. Just what he gave me for gluttony alone — if the Feds were that strict you wouldn't hardly see any bankers or murderers walking around on the streets. And the impure thoughts, especially the really *stupid* impure thoughts, with like mung all over 'em, and the sticky icky impure deeds ... Plus all those cars I borrowed, though I always usually brought 'em back.

But the worst, it turns out — Joey had it about right — the worst was what I did to Nico. I told the Father how it was all in a good cause, how it frankly — don't wanna blow m'own horn here, but — frankly took a good lot o' guts to do it, seeing as who Nico is and how I generously left him alive; and how really I'd just been doing everybody a big favor, you know — not that I was asking for any *thanks* or anything, always happy to oblige — and how I'd planned right from the git-go to come and confess it, and now here I am, you satisfied? do I get a receipt?; but he isn't buying it. He is silent for a long while. While I sit and sweat and squirm. Then he gives me absolution for the other stuff, along with a lot of homework, Hooray Marys and like that, for all the *other* stuff: but *not for that*.

This I had not been expecting at all. I'm dumbfounded. What am I supposed to do *now*, I ask; I already confessed it! He says: You have to repent. Yeh well, I'm *sorry*, okay? — He's not buying it: You don't have to apologize, you have to repent. — And now I'm really facing a quandary here because, now that I look at it, I haven't repented that at all: fact, really kind of pleased the way it all worked out, me thinking on my feet, getting in a nice right hook, and then Nico (who had it coming anyway) opening up like that. I mean Murphy you are really one tough swift son-of-a ... whoops, sorry, forgetting where I am. — So how do I do *that*? I ask. — He says: It happens by Grace. — And I say, O-*kay*, Grace, got it, I'll make a note, but … if it happens, how will I know that the Grace, like, *took*? I mean, no point taking another hour out of my busy schedule and blowing five bucks on a cab, just to come back here for nothing, waste of time. I mean it's like an inoculation — how do I know that the repentance is real? — You'll know, he said.

So I come out of it like from a wringer that's been set for Heavy Load, and Ground-In Dirt, and after all that I still got this big ugly blotchy stain right on my soul-front. I drag myself to a bar and order a milk.

I finally got home around midnight. Joey still waiting up.

"Ja go?"

"Yeh, I went. But I flunked."

Joey's amazed. "How do you *flunk*, *Confession*??"

"It's my soul, Joey. It's like the inside of a garbage can. It's like a leper what got the clap. It's like the rear-end of a wart-hog that got the runs."

"Yeh I know that, Murphy, but those guys are supposed to be good at those hopeless cases. They're pros. Really gets off the grease and grime."

"Yeh well, they spiffed me up a little. New plugs and points. But you were right about the hand thing, Joey, turns out."

"Oh — ya mean you're sorry for it now, now you've had time and thought about it?"

"No Joey, that's just the problem. I mean it's hard to be sorry for something after, when you weren't sorry before."

"O-oh, Murphy, that's bad."

We sit around awhile glumly, not talking. Then he looks up kind of sly. "I'll bet they really nailed ya on the gluttony stuff, huh."

"Oh yeh, they gave me some homework. I told 'em all about it."

"Even the Chocolate Chewums?"

"Even the Chocolate Chewums."

Joey lets out a whistle, which kind of grates on me.

"You gotta admit, though, I don't put on much fat."

"True, Murphy, you somehow sleep it off."

So we're smiling, we're friends again.

"I kept your dinner hot, Murphy," he grins. "You getting in so late."

"So, what's for dinner, Joey?"

"Pop-tarts and spinach, I'd planned on, only ...."

"All out of spinach again, eh?"

"Y-ep."

Chapter Four

The stuff Nico knew, I could've stayed up all night listening to him, sitting around the campfire; but those were other cases, other times.

What he told me about the LaBelle business was sketchy, but enough to keep us busy, though it didn't really make sense.

His orders, he thinks, came ultimately from the top of the Scabroso mob that works out of Florida. He *thinks* the top; but the cut-outs sometimes boast a little. They wanted him to find anything at all about Richie Mallow that he can dig up in LaBelle's apartment. Richie, it seems, was essentially a free agent, but he'd been on-and-off partners with them till recently, but then he either ripped them off, or someone made it seem like he ripped them off, anyhow he's made himself scarce and they can't ask him. And whether he did or whether he didn't, either way he knows way too much. They'd already figured out she had no idea where he is, which wasn't hard, and which explains why she wasn't roughed up any — apart from being killed, I mean. But they figured she might have been in possession something she didn't know about, which would have been way likely except that Richie was so careful.

The next piece doesn't fill any gaps but creates new ones; it might be a piece of a different puzzle. There's this Morsue mob, works out of Marseille. Now, rightly or wrongly, the Scabrosos somehow got it into their head that the French gang was onto Mallow in some way — had their hooks in him, or knew stuff about him that they didn't — anyhow they didn't like it. He was very useful as a kind of semi-legitimate front, and any dirt or any publicity or any anything could mess that up right away. Do the French guys want to buy him, blackmail him, or ice the guy — the Scabrosos don't know, but it's bad any way you turn it.

Then finally, they said, terminate the lady. Why? Cause it's one of two things. *One*: She put him up to it, this powder he took. Then it's retribution. Or, *two*: the guy just took a powder and left her in the lurch. Which means she'll get miffed off and maybe squeal all she knows. Now, as for Mallow, that's *his* look-out; but the guy's got friends, and enemies of friends, who do not want their laundry, with its unsightly stains, blowing about in plain sight.

The hardest part was the message in her phonebook. I knew he hadn't seen it or he would've taken it with him. But maybe he could tell me what it meant. Only, I didn't want to add it to the stuff *he* knew, I just wanted to add what he knew to what *I* knew, so I let it ride. The thing is, the only way I'm gonna get out in front is by knowing more than the other mugs. I'm not smarter, stronger, faster, or braver. And I'm a whole lot uglier. The only thing going for me, is what I know.

As to how he managed to get in there so silent, and ice her so nice, well, it's all in the wrist, he couldn't even hardly explain it.

I lay all this out to Joey real proud of all I got, but he just sits there and mopes. Maybe partly account of he's prejudiced, it being ill-gotten gains, but mostly he says it don't lead nowhere except up Sheet Creek.

"Look," he says, "now we're into mobsters. And mobsters, man, they're always going at each other and breaking the china and it's bye-bye bystanders along the way. None of that tells us a thing about Mallow. The guy could be crooked, the guy might be straight. Or just a little shady, like sometimes you 'n' me. Might've just crossed their path. Those guys they hear a rumor, they don't hire a historian, they just act on it, on impulse, doesn't mean it makes any sense. And Mallow could still be anywhere. Fact, simple fact they did that, means they have no idea either."

I had to admit he had a point there. "So whadawe do next?"

Joey looks at me pained; he knows I'm not going to like what he got to say. "Y'know, Murphy, good brother: I know ya don't like to admit it when we're licked, but fact is, when we started on this case, we were down one missing man and up one client, and now we're down both. And his footprints disappear into a swamp of mobsters. Nobody's gonna pay us, all it's gonna do is cost us, I'll have to hock my wad of gum that I'm not

69

even done with it yet, and all for what? Murphy — what say we just ... drop this case."

Everything he says is true, but still, no way. "Detectives don't drop cases, Joey."

"Murphy, this case dropped *us*."

"No go, Joey. We're in this too deep."

Joey's jaw dropped. "Too *deep*, we ain't even in shallow! We're nowhere, just south of no-place-at-all. Mallow's having breakfast with the Man in the Moon, for all we know, our client died — there's nothing left to even be deep *in*."

"I know that, Joey, but don't forget. I committed a sin to get into this, a raw red sin that it ain't been forgiven. It's like an ulcer where my soul ought to be. I got to follow through, Joey, I just got to, follow it through and run it down and work it out."

Joey looks at me like a rhino looks when it's feeling tender. "Aww, good brother, ya don't gotta do all that. Ya just gotta repent and — bingo! You're in the clear."

"I know that too. But what I don't know is how to do that. You can't just ... *repent*, it's not like turning on a faucet. I tried it and it's dry; nothing comes out. So what I'm gonna do is what I do know how to do."

He asked me what that was.

"Rattle the cages, stir the pot! Shake the trees for leads! Follow 'em wherever they take us. And look, we already got one. Lookit this."

I show him the note that came out of the phonebook. He reads it carefully.

70

"All right, so she was gonna meet a friend at the Lido come Friday. Two p.m. — you don't have to spell that out, I'm a detective, it means afternoon. Only looks like she won't be making it."

"But we will."

He looks startled. "What's the point? She's gone now, that won't bring her back. And you wanna find out more about her, be my guest, she didn't make any big secret out of her life like he did, there's tons of people we could talk to. Heck, call up her mom if you want. Interview her kindergarten teacher. You can write a best-seller, *The LaBelle that I Knew*. — And anyhow, we don't know what her friend looks like or the name."

"Well, I don't calculate as how it's a friend she just might've been seeing for fun."

"How you figure?"

"Look, she sees her girlfriends all the time. Saw. How she makes appointments or remembers them is anybody's guess — maybe same-time-same-place, maybe just kept it in her head, maybe a memo book that Nico made off with. But there was *only one note* in the phonebook. Whoever made the call, for whatever it was, it was unexpected, not her routine. Maybe a friend with something urgent; more likely a stranger. And a stranger with something pretty interesting, her to say Okay I'll see ya, sight unseen, just over the phone."

"I follow you, Murphy. So who — wait, lemme play shamus. Right here — a clue, a clue! It says, 'pink'. Now, who wears pink? *Dames*, Murphy, even I know that. She was gonna meet a dame, a stranger, and the way to recognize her, she'll be wearing pink."

"Only problem is, *lotsa* dames wear pink. It wouldn't pick her out. The way I see it, it'll be a guy."

Joey recoils. "A *guy*, Murphy, wearing *pink*? That's not normal."

"Joey, there's a lotta guys out there more'n what you see out of the end of your beer-glass. Some of 'em wears pink. And some could do it, just once, for a specific purpose. Doesn't mean a whole pink suit or anything, too noticeable; and not a pink shirt, not noticeable enough — there might be another one. I say a pink tie or — hold it Joey, I got it. Pink socks!"

He looks at me funny. "Pink ... socks ?"

"Yeh Joey look, it's brilliant. He's walking around, trouser cuffs down, nobody sees 'em. Then he sits ina café, dame walks in that it could be her, or that he knows it's her, and he crosses one leg up over the other, just sittin'ere sippin'is coffee, real natural, and as soon as she spots it, he sees her reaction and puts it down. Nobody else would even need to see it."

"Yeh it's a neat idea, Murphy. Wonder if the guy is smart enough to of thought of it too."

"We'll find out Friday.

So we got a day to wait, and it sets in to raining. Joey's catching up on his comic books. Me I'm checking out the funny papers, see what old Popeye is up to; maybe work up to a crossword, maybe not. Only first I do my homework — fifty Hail Mary's every day for a week. I don't have a rosary, so I'm racking them up on the counters over the pool table.

After a couple of hours of this, Joey starts getting antsy and even Little Audrey can't cheer him up. So he heads on over to Sammy's for the gerbil races, got nothing in his pocket right now for a bet, but maybe they'll give him credit. Only don't bet on *that*.

So I'm fishing around in the papers I already read, done all the crosswords as far as I could do 'em, reading about recent guys that died, only none with a bearing on this case. And now I'm out of stuff to read.

Well okay here's the puzzle page. It's called "The Sixty-Four Dollar Question", and it tries to stump the readers, then gives the answers. Any number can play. And today's stumper goes like this:

WHAT ... is the 'Unpardonable Sin'?

Never heard of it but it makes my skin crawl, just the same — just the name. Kind of thing I would've learned in catechism if I'd gone parochial instead of first public and then hooky and then reform. Even as it is, I know enough from just what I picked up in the gutter, to know that it's not one of the first things that might come to mind, like rooting for the Yankees, or having it off with your own mom or anything like that. I chew a pencil-end for a minute, see if I can suck it somehow out of the wood, then I give up and turn to page 54.

If you answered, "Despair", give yourself half credit. The correct answer is: Blasphemy against the Holy Spirit.

Uh-oh.

My blood runs cold. Could I of done that? Not real likely — I can sin up a storm but I do watch my tongue. But even worse, what about Joey? He's a sweet guy but he does have a temper sometimes, specially if he misses breakfast. Hits his thumb with a hammer or loses a Pop-tart behind the sink, and he blasphemes like nobody's business, cussing something awful, mostly yapping on about the First and Second Persons, but who knows, maybe one time he got extra hot under the collar and was running out of G-words and J-words, he might've just gone and clipped one to the Ghost. Mighta done it, mighta not. — Never did hear him messing over the Virgin, though.

Jeez — I mean Jeepers, this looks bad. My own brother, maybe even me! Cause it doesn't say: Badmouthing the Spirit over sixty times, like a speed-limit, or even ten. It says: *Just once, Jack*, near as I can tell. And —"unpardonable" — do they really mean that? can they? Is that even possible? A buddy can pardon you anything if he feels like it, or you fork him a fiver or whatnot, so they must mean it's God who's doing the pardoning or not pardoning. And it sounds like in this case even He can't do it, infinite mercy be blowed.

Joey's out, and I'm alone, and I start to panic. He could get run over by a pie truck or something, in a state of ... This is awful. I think of calling up a priest, then I remember my name is mud with those guys. But I just got to find out the facts.

Right, right! The public library. Haven't been there that much since I was a kid, that anatomy book. I hop in my wheels and burn rubber, park next to a hydrant right in front of the place and burst up the steps. Lady behind the desk looks like she been weaned on a lemon but when I ask Where's the *Catholic Encyclopedia* she loosens up a little and points to a shelf.

I look in the U's, *Unpardonable Sin*. Nothing. Not even tellya where to look. I mean what if it's an emergency? which it is. — I try another volume. *Sin, cooperation in*. Oh yeh, me and Joey done that. — *Sin, desert of*. Oo-oogh, this is awful, didn't even know there was such a place but what if we're going around the world in a balloon and it crashes and that's where we wind up? — *Sin against the Holy Spirit*. Hey wait a minute, this is it!

I read it in a fever.

"Unlike all other sins and blasphemies (Mk 3.28), the blasphemy against the Holy Spirit' ... is characterized by Jesus as unforgivable."

What — *He* said that, the meek and mild? Not just some crazy preacher? Oh, this is really bad. I feel dizzy, coming over sick, I put my head down on the desk.

My moans bring over the librarian. "Are you alright … sir?" she inquires, not very tenderly. I shake my head on my folded arms. "Do you need a doctor?" I croak: "It's gone past that." She looks down at what I'm reading, and starts back in alarm. "Do you — do you need a priest?"

I lift my head up, all sweaty and covered with pizza shavings. "In the worst way, but I don't dare see one. They got me top of their blip-list. It's like — you know how you feel when you get your monthlies? My soul — it's all unclean!"

She recoils, and hurries off. Probably thinking that what I really need is a policeman. I hurry to read the rest.

Saint Augustine, it says, "understood the irremissibility to be absolute." I push on, groaning, reading it like a cancer report. But then it says; "Now the only sin to which absolute irremissibility can be attributed is final impenitence; even God cannot forgive the unrepented sin, and this Augustine understood to be the sin against the Holy Spirit."

Deeper and downer, worse and worse.

But then hope like a mole pokes its nose up through the rubble.

"... sins that are unforgiveable only in the sense that they put an obstacle in the way of forgiveness, but they do not make its attainment impossible because the obstacle is not such that it cannot be overcome by the grace of God."

That's it! It's the final impenitence! Nothing to do with cussing! The rest is just metaphorical stuff from like English class! Joey's in the clear.

Only, uh-oh, *I'm* not. I reread it: *"Even God cannot forgive an unrepented sin."* And I got one, O do I got one. Remember that little outstanding spiritual traffic ticket, Murphy? Five bucks won't fix it, nor five million neither, this Judge cannot be bought.

Have I repented yet? It's hard to say; I try feeling around in my soul like a doctor palpating for tumors. Nope, doesn't feel like it; heck that rat Nico got what he deserved. Does this mean I'll be joining him where it looks like he's going? I keep reading:

*"... unforgiveable only in the sense that no extenuating circumstance appealed to the divine mercy for forgiveness; but this by no means made it impossible for the divine mercy **to move the sinner gratuitously to repentance and so to pardon**."*

Oh Lord ... Please Lord ... move me gratuitously, move me all you please. Move me to the desert and dump me there. Move me to the moon, to the ends of the earth, move me to the pit and the mountains of ice, to the blackness of night and the fire of flame. Move me, Lord, move me. Let me be turned on a spit, and burnt to a crisp, if it be Thy pleasure; only so, that the sin be burned away with me. Fling me out among the stars and let me drift there in the dark, through the cold and the void, for a billion stretches of centuries, if that is what must be; while I repent as slowly slowly, as the winking-out of stars: yet only, let it be, that may I drift ... to Thee.

I close the book and am shuffling off in chains, just as the security guard comes reluctantly over, the librarian bustling along a few feet behind him and egging him on. He looks at me doubtfully, me in my busted-up t-shirt and all; but he's got a bit of a stubble himself. And a bit of a paunch. And a kind of a wine-map on the veins of his face, showing all the places he's driven or been driven to, drinking; and all the sadness he has saddened to, thinking; and all the shame he's had to swallow, hat in hand till he could get this part-time job flung to him like a slab of meat, this chilly charity, this dead-end gig as a security-guard — not even a mall guard or a construction site, just a library security-guard, lowest of the low, kids snicker at him, fiction's over that way ma'am, rest rooms one floor down. He goes home alone to his SRO and he thinks upon the day, so much like yesterday, so much like tomorrow and the days after that. And a look inside his eyes, way deep down, you have to squint almost to even see it, that is sad past sadness, and deep past depth, like pennies at the bottom of a dried-up well.

I reach out and shake his hand, then hold it for a while. He doesn't speak, but he looks at me, and slowly his eyes form pools, that once-dry well is filling up, the tears are almost like hope, so wet and fruitful, reaching the brim and finally overflowing, gushing forth like a flood, watering that blank stretching desert of sin, until the flowers come up and the cactuses bloom, and the sun spins in the sky and the stars wheel around like hamsters on a wheel, and the ghosts float up from out their tombs, and the beggar gets his rusk at last, and the heavens crack and the rain pours down, washing it all away, the sins and the sadness and the pain and the badness, and somehow now we're embracing, he and I, how did that happen, we're like boxers in a clinch, hugging so hard and staggering, and I can't even tell his own tears from mine.

At last I say — meaning it: "You're going to be okay."

"*I know*," he says. And we part.

Chapter Five

Friday arrives. Sunlight streaming in, right through the blinds. We pull them back, and the sky blazes blue like a squadron of trumpets. Bouncing off the buildings like machinegun fire. Fireplugs like bonfires, parked cars like elephants of war. Sidewalks like Persian carpets, fire-escapes like escaping fire. The meter-maid in her plastic-wrapped cap and her transparent raincoat, despite the nice day. She is writing in her little notebook, scribbling furiously her notebook, writing a love-letter, yes I'm sure of it, she is writing a love letter to the owner of that Buick parked at a fireplug like a bonfire of war, tribes dancing around it in full battledress in our minds, writing words she could never bring herself to express in real life, writing pages and pages upon pages of words — O thou who drivest this noble Buick, resting its weary wheels beside this fireplug here, how can we ever give adequate thanks for this beautiful day. Fare forth, in thy bright blue Buick, the klaxon blaring, announcing the arrival, announcing the good news. And how deeply it doth pain me, to be obliged to write thee this parking ticket here! — The sun shines laughing; the streets laugh, shining. *Everything* ... shines, in the sun.

In sum: A great day to lounge around at the Lido; while somewhere, elsewhere, in their ill-lit holes, the last remaining taxpayers do the actual work of the nation: staving off, for a time, that reckoning-day, when the whole hollow jerrybuilt structure collapses in dust around our ears.

The Lido is what passes for a Sicilian place, on the east side, run by Greeks. It's got round white metal tables out front, on a big terrace with pennants and Italian flags; and parasols, colored like every hue of fruit candy, which you can tilt so as to have, to your liking, sun or shade. A wrought-iron railing runs around the outside edge of the terrace, geometrical and dignified, with just enough detailing to give it heart. A green-and-white striped awning projects over the back half, so that those who wish some privacy for a heart-to-heart can have it, while those who want to see and be seen throne gloriously at the forecastle, high overlooking the sidewalks, where those who toil, and those who labor, trudge unseeing unfeelingly by.

The Lido — it's got what you want. They got espresso, in demitasses like flower cups; plus regular coffee for normal people; and tiny little cakes, look like miniature treasure chests and cost as much; and leetle teensy colored drinks, all the colors of the rainbow, in eensy glasses — dames can't get enough of such stuff — but the management won't chew you out, or throw you out, if you just order a beer. Acourse, they mostly got beer from across the sea. Which I don't mind, actually some of them taste almost as good as what my grandpa took for granted, back in Milwaukee, back in the day; and way much better than the diluted-down piss-lemonade that's been passing for beer ever since Satan bought up all the breweries and then sold them on to some Volstead-Act ninety-year-old virgin that hates beer and hates men who are men ... Heck one of them imports is like drinking two beers at once — of course, for the price of six, but who's counting, nobody's counting, the toffs got their cash and the business types their expense accounts — and for the rest of us, it's a beautiful day. Plus they got steaks, and veal, with foreign words after it, and a kind of like Lebanese pizza.

All sorts of people come here, all walks of life. Some on foot, some on bicycle, some in rickshaw or on horseback; some in taxis, some in chauffeured limousines. Some in handcuffs, some in tux; some in yachts drawn down the middle of the street by a team of white horses, some in big blue balloons that hover against the sun while they rappel down by rope ladder; some in spaceships or UFOs. Rich guys and poor guys; women looking for rich guys, rich guys looking for easygoing not-rich women, not-rich guys looking exquisitely like rich guys and looking for rich women so that they can be rich guys for real; and some reserved and unaccompanied reasonably though usually not excessively rich guys, looking to pick up a waiter. All kinds, you can find them, right here at the Lido. Welcome — to my world.

(And again, the briefest fugue, a kind of blackout, and yet still standing, at least I am standing when, an instant later, I wake up. And again a kind of piece of a slice of a vision of things.

I walk haltingly, arms out front, feeling the way, like a blind man, and of course I am blind. I walk for the longest time, gently stumbling in the dark, and then come up with a bump, against — something. And I feel it, feelingly feel it, all over with my happy hands, running them lovingly over the rich infinite textures, stone, crumbled, like stucco; and this — this could even be brick! most beloved brick! O God how I love it, this beautiful brick — its sharp hard chips, as my hands begin to bleed.)

We stow the Pontiac in a no-parking zone since it's registered to some other guy anyway, and stroll over to the café. Blank stares staring back at us from behind blank tell-nothing sunglasses or maybe staring past over our heads. We're trudging up the broad stone steps when Joey nudges me. A woman, sitting near the railing, alone. Blonde, a little zaftig, but a decent figure all the same . "Nice, Joey, nice."

But he nudges me again, and side-mouths a hot whisper. "The *dress*, Murphy, the *dress*."

And I look and oh right: a pink dress. "You still got that theory, Joey? All right, keep an eye on her." But then her escort comes back from inside where he just settled up. He leaves a tip on the table and they leave together.

"Just goes to show, Joey. Pink — it's like a plague."

We pick out a table at the rear of the terrace, next to the door to the inside part of the restaurant, where mostly just old people eat. From here we can survey the whole scene.

It's almost 1:30, and the terrace is almost full — lunch hour starts late here, and it's a beautiful day. People lounging around, working hard on their tans, flogging their expense accounts, sipping tall cool drinks or sweet small drinks, pinkies raised or kept in waiting, picking birdlike at salads got up like ballerinas, or dishes with pineapple stuck on 'em to remind you of another country; chatting, looking sexy, sitting back, striking poses; dreaming of Babylon, buying or selling, making deals. Waiters in short tight jackets with faces like masks glide by as though on roller-skates, weaving in and out, expressionless as flamenco dancers, the dancers and the dance.

"Crikes, it's the middle of a workday," I mutter. "Who *are* all these people? Don't nobody got a *job* anymore?"

"There's the waiters," suggests Joey.

"Pfah, most of 'em are dealing, or selling their flesh, or else just killing time till they can get a movie deal." I grimace at them as they glide by like butlers on magnetic levitation.

One slides up and we order a pair of beers.

Joey's looking around, nervous. Not the kind of place we generally hang out, at all. Place is really getting on his nerves. "Looks suspicious, Murphy."

"How so, Joey?" He's never been here before, and, truth to tell, he doesn't get out much.

"Well like — just fr'instance — get a load a *that* guy." He doesn't dare point, but he nods the direction.

A tall thin customer, very tan above his blinding-white shirt, with a copper-colored suit, and wavy black hair with a hint at the temples of an interest in the silver market. He is sipping a greenish liquid and gazing off into some inner distance.

"Like, what *race* is he even. Features, you'd say a white guy. But he's some other color, not exactly brown but like some kind of metal. And it's only the beginning of June."

"He gets it from the snow, Joey, skiing; and from the glare off the water, in boats; and from tanning salons. That way they get to keep that hot-dog color all year round."

"An'at guy there, it's like he got boobs."

"That's a lady, Joey, she just cut her hair."

"An'at — what's widd*at* guy."

"That's a yuppie, Joey, be gentle with him. He cannot help the way he is."

The beers arrive, at last we have something we both understand. At the table next to us, two broads swish in and flounce down and one studies the menu and one studies her nails. A waiter quickly whispers by, and bows to hear what their pleasure might be; but he could have spared the effort, cause their voices are like a foghorn. One of them orders a *banana dikery* and Joey flushes right up to his ears (turning them *pink* — if he could see them, he'd suspect *himself*); he cannot believe what they just said. The other orders a *pink lady* and now it's my turn to do a double-take. This could be more complicated than I thought.

The minutes tick by and we're scoping out the terrace. Two o'clock approaches like a locomotive in a silent movie. Drinks are being swallowed, deals are going down, people are falling in lust like flies.

A very young couple is sitting holding hands and looking around them; this is probably a splurge for them, a first date. A portly guy, alone, opens another button on his vest, which vainly attempts to cover the sort of grease build-up that is laid on carefully layer by layer, meal after gourmand meal. An unescorted woman comes up the stairs and he raises his glass to her, a sapphire on his little finger winking in the sun. But she walks right by him and sits down with another group.

We order another round of beers to help us think. This vendor guy with flowers is making his rounds. He pauses at our table. "Buttonholes, gentlemen?"

Joey looks down at his shirt. "My buttons is already got holes."

The vendor doesn't blink an eye or miss a beat, he's already walking off, softly chanting. "Buttonholes, anyone? Chrysanthemums, carnations, pinks?"

Joey starts from his chair. "what'd he say?"

"We'll keep an eye on him, Joey."

We crane our necks and grab a scoop of the conversation going on at the next table. A couple of businessmen are griping about labor conditions.

"And now they're talking *union*, I swear to God. God damned bunch of pinkos."

"Yeh but it's the distaff that gets to me," says his companion, "the pink-collar workers. Always wanting maternity leave and equal wages and —"

A woman at a nearby table raises her voice in laughter and it cuts in. "Marj, you would *not* believe. I was tickled pink! He just —"

A swirl of chatter blows in on the breeze, wafting this way and that "— and the poor child comes down with pinkeye and —"/ "imagine how dreary it can get, out there on the Cape, the raindrops going pink pink pink on the tin roof all-"/ "Aww, *Playboy*'s a wimp sheet. Now you take the *Penthouse*. *They* were the first to show pink."

"Roderick!" shouts a fellow to a new arrival. "My but you're looking in the pink of health!"

"— and then she stabs him with the pinking shears and — -"

Joey jumps up, looking wildly around. "Waiter! Bring me a double whiskey! Make that two!"

The waiter smiles and chuckles. "You keep going like that, this early in the day, you'll be seeing pink elephants by sunset."

Me I'm paying no attention. Folks don't realize —
once you start getting your antennae up, for something
like that, you generally find it. (Like, here; simple
experiment: *Walrus*. **Walrus** !!! It's the key to the
Meaning of Life! It's the key to the freaking
Intergalactic Conspiracy!!!! **WALRUS**!!! — Now see if
you don't start finding walruses under every bed. [Hey
there's one now ....]) But Joey, he's freaking; the man is
freaking out. Kind of surprises me, because, usually,
you got faith — it's like you're full, you got no more
room for superstitions. Well, give him a break, the man
is out of his element, he is seriously out of his depth
here, all these bankers and hookers, these hookers and
bankers, — these banker-hookers and hooker-bankers,
with red rims on their eyes, and the credit-cards
flashing, blood rushing blindly to their private parts ....
But me I take it easy. World's got all kinda stuff, I give
it a pass — and that's just *this* planet, *here*. Who knows
what the Martians might be up to.

So I'm lookinaroun', and I'm lookinaroun' ... and
now I do see something that interests me. A pudgy guy
who's been looking nervously this way and that, the
whole time he's been here, periodically wiping his brow
with a red-white pocket kerchief like it's the center of
summer — although, really, today, it's cool for June —
(and wait, think about it: red plus white over two,
equals pink) now he looks at his watch, scowls, leaves a
wad of payment on the table, stands up to his full
(short) height, begins to walk off; finds his shoe is

untied, and stoops to tie it. He's like a classic Greek statue, there on the terrace, against the light — Olympian stoops, to adjust his sandal. And as he does so — less Greek and less heroically — his pant leg rides up.

I slap Joey on the upper arm. "*Lookit*, Joey!" I hiss-whisper; "There it is! Pink *socks*!"

The guy has finished with his shoes and is heading down the steps at a brisk waddle. I leave a flourish of bills on the table, and we hustle after him. It's a routine we've done before, Joey'n me; got it down like a buck-and-wing. I come up to the left of him, Joey comes up on the right, we each grab an elbow at the same time with one hand and start whopping him hard on the back with the other.

"*Wally* old pal! Where you been hiding yourself?" Lurching and laughing, Joey's thumping him so hard he can hardly squawk back, saying (top of his lungs) "Say hey, *Wally* baby! Long time no see!" Meanwhile we steer him over into our car.

"Unhand me!" he gurgles, but we're laughing and shouting and I gun the engine real loud. The car starts off and we drive till we're out of earshot of anyone who might've seen us — and all at once, the shouts and the laughter are gone. Just driving silently down deserted streets towards the outskirts of town.

Now his eyes get wide and the sweat pearls on his forehead like these beautiful tiny BB's from a BB-gun. He begins to yelp and whimper. "Nonono please;

please; where are you taking me. P- P- Pl — *Please*. I will do anything. You want I pleasure you? — No; no, I can see that, scratch that, no pleasure you." Joey and I seemingly not even listening, staring bored straight ahead. "Look — here — I have — a little money tucked away — it isn't much, and it's not *on* me, only ... Here, what's in my wallet, it isn't much, but take it please take it: please. It is all that I have. All that is left to me. I offer it to you — I'm on my knees — I *want* you to have it. Yes! Even if you were to let me go right now: I would *want* you to have it — the wallet (genuine imitation leather) and everything in it, you are such gentlemen, I honor you, O please, allow me to honor you; take my wallet, take my clothes, take whatever remains of my dignity, but — Leave me, O I beg of you, Leave me ... with my life."

I slow the car down. "Your life, huh? Sounds like the one you got is kinda complicated. You sure you want to keep the one you got?"

He stares at the question; but it's a reasonable question; and to answer it, he returns to a reasonable tone. "My life is a mess, that much is obvious. But I'd like to have the chance to try to make something out of it, nevertheless. Maybe I might someday to something that isn't totally gross. Not likely — but I do have hope."

All at once I'm really liking the guy, queer though he seems. And the idea of his being the mysterious Mr. Pink. is seeming seriously unlike: this customer is just

91

not tough enough. Still, I got to pump him a little, my duty as a detective.

"Relax, buddy, " I say, "we're taking you to L.L." LaBelle LeBaron, if he's in this at all.

His eyes like saucers. "*El Al*? Oh no — you're terrorists ...."

"L. *L.* As in: LaBelle."

He just stares; lips flapping wind. Nothing registers.

"The dame that you come here to meet."

He gives a hiccup, wrapped in a giggle. "A ... a ... *dame*?! Me?" He suffers a brief bout of hysterics. "Oh yes, you're right, gentlemen, plead guilty — me! — I did, you've got my number; I did come here, to meet: a *dame* ...."

I look at him funny. "Does this dame have a name?"

"Why — why yes! My fiancée! Ha-ha! What a — *dame*, as you say!"

"Her name, her name."

"Her ... name? I ... don't remember ...." I grab his neck in my pinching fingers. "Yes! I remember now. Silly, me forgetting. It's Judy. Beautiful Judy. But she didn't show. Might have been delayed. Well, no matter, I'll get another. Oh my yes."

The car slows to a stop, idling beside a poplar that, although it's June, has already lost all its leaves. This sounds like it's going nowhere, but I make one last stab. I jab a pencil up next to his belly-button. "The dame's name is LaBelle, as you know damn well. And

you got two seconds to tell us her last name or this
stiletto dipped in Amazonian toad-poison is going
deep-deep into your rotten gut."

His eyelids just peel right back from his eyes, and
he starts in jabbering. "Her — Smith! It's Smith! No?
Miller — that's right, Miller! — Wrong? Oh right:
Williams; it's Williams; Williams for sure. W-Williams?
no Williams? ... It's ... *Brown. Brown*, I tell you. No —
Green. Sloan! Ramirez! — No no ouch, don't do that, I
still have a second left, it's — O'Donnell, Rostropovich,
MacGillicuddy, McNamara ... It's Eliott — Eliott! Eliott
with one L and two T's — no, Elliot with two L's and
one T — no, just one each ... two each ... please ...."
Then all names melt into a mess inside his mouth, and
his fat frame heaves with sobs.

I sigh, I pat him on the back. "Sorry, pardner. *A
gaze of mizdagen i-denidy.* Here's a twenty for your
time," I shove a Jackson into his pocket. "Cheer up —
chin up. Have a nice life." I open the door and give a
gentle shove; he stumbles off.

We've already come about a mile beyond the Lido
when I remember I left my shades on the table. We
turn around, drive back, park next to a vacant hydrant,
and walk back up.

And just as we're heading up the steps, the well-
oiled party with the gem on his hand is picking his
teeth and ambling down off the deck. He nicks his head

to one side, motioning me and Joey, to a waiting limousine.

Anything for kicks. But first things first. I hold up a significant index finger, a gesture he respects, and go towards our former table, which now has five people at it. The waiter beaming meets me with my shades, with a big smile as well he might, since that hasty payment cleaned me out, and even when you subtract off for the pricey beers, it must've been one helluva tip. Then I head back down, not in a hurry, and walk on to just a little bit past the guy's car; where I pause, scrutinizing my watch, and flicking it with my finger like maybe it's stopped.

"I like your action, my little friends," he murmurs from the dark inside, window rolled just partway down. "Very smooth, the way you nabbed that guy."

"What guy," I say in a monotone, to my watch.

"Fatso, your long lost friend."

"Oh him," says Joey, "we hadda talk over old times."

"Short talk," he observes. "Already you're back."

"Yeh well, *you* know, ya run outa things to say. Like, How's the *wife*, how's the *kids*, how's the *cat*, how's the *dog*, how's the *car* ...."

"And that was your mistake. Guys like that don't *have* wives, and their family's ashamed of 'em, which means no ransom, or not as much. Wasted effort."

"Oh hey now look you think we —"

"Can it. I got a job for you both."

We get in.

We drive awhile without talking, just taking in the scenic countryside; Joey in the front seat, me in the back. Buildings going by; then billboards; then trees.

And then he starts in with the small-talk. "You guys are not mobbed up; that's obvious." Me and Joey — mum's the word. "You're amateurs — but you got an instinct. I like that." He nods appreciatively; and then he shakes his head, not liking something else. "There's too many teams on the field right now. Like a checkerboard with too many pieces — no-one can jump." We nod assent, not knowing what the heck he's talking about, but we're being good guests. "Fact is," he goes on, "I could use some independents — guys without a record — independents who are working for *me*."

We let this sink in. Me and Joey we exchange a look. Me and Joey we exchange a shrug. So then me — mostly I do the talking: "And who might this '*me*' be?"

Still driving, he half-turned in his seat. Big grin. "Curiosity — very bad. Axed the cat." He turned back to his driving but chattered on. "But hey, if you do want a handle, you can call me: Brown. — *Mis*-ter Brown!" And he threw back his head and just: laughed, and laughed, and laughed.

Already I am thinking: Brown is not coming to my birthday party.

By now the nicer parts of town were far behind.

We'd passed through a section full of derelicts, like a vacant lot with weeds; and a landscape of abandoned factories, plangent with the ghosts of lost jobs; and now things were thinning out, to where there weren't even any derelicts, just boarded-up windows and wisps of rags, and faded signs of businesses that had failed, gone bust, *oh*, so long ago .... And then finally, we are within smelling-distance, of the docks.

He stops the car in the middle of the street. No traffic — no need to pull over to where the curb would be, if there were a curb.

"You get out here," he says to me. "And the big guy—" He jerks a thumb. "Whacher name, Big Guy?"

"Bruto," says Joey.

"Yeh, well uh, Bruto; your brother is coming with me. And you," turning to me, "your job, ahh ... —"

"Sir Percy la Fifi the Third," I say, with a straight face.

"Right." (Not missing a beat.) "Your job, Purse, is to memorize this message. Gotcha grey-cells goin'? This message:

"Target a no-show. Cut bait."

He paused. "Repeat it." I did. Word-perfect, like a little schoolboy.

"Good. So now you take that message and you give it to the man who will answer a certain door. On this door — a green door — you will knock precisely four times; and then you will wait ... wa-it ... and then knock again just once. Then no more knocking, and you wait as long as it takes. Might take a minute, might take a thousand years. Not your business. You just wait there. A statue of stone. And when at last that green door opens, opens wide, the light flooding out, you tell him "Mister B. sent me" and then you give him the message. — You remember the message?"

I recite, like a lad in knickerbockers: "*Target a no-show. Cut bait.*"

"Good; good; very good. And then he's happy and he gives you a lollipop: a nice, red, lollipop."

(I'm not liking this guy, I'm not liking this guy; not my birthday; not my bar-mitzvah either ....)

"Then he might give you a message for me; or he might not. Life is so unpredictable — don't you think? But either way, you report right back to the shed here, right next to where we're parked, right now — it might be bright of day, or dark of night; you come here, carrying your message."

"Carrying my message."

"In your two twin hands, like hot soup in a bowl, that you don't want to spill. You got it?"

"I — get it. But. This is a lot of walking and talking and waiting. They say money talks but I ain't heard it talking. It'd better pipe up."

A smile spreads over his face like butter on a pancake. Curiosity he's allergic; but greed he understands. Big smile on his pancake face.

"Here's a fifty to keep your pocket warm. And the left half of a couple of hundreds; other halves when you're done. Same goes for this bozo with the fake name Bruto — so double anything I said."

"All right," I say, indifferently pocketing the bill. "I reckon this'll keep us in pizza. So where do I got to go?"

"You just head right on down that side-street, till you come to a green door. It looks boarded-up but it isn't, just pull on it, out and up." He pointed a fat forefinger towards the place in question, and again I see the dark ring glinting on his pinky. "Head on in, it's dark, that don't bother you I hope, till you come to the end of the corridor. Feel around till you find smooth wood, then knock like I told you: four times; pause; once."

"Will do."

I ducked out of the car and gave a halfway salute good-bye. He raised his left hand till the thumb touched his brow, then sort of flicked it out and said, for some reason, "Chow." Which is just what I could use about now, but something else just struck me about this pudgy snappy guy with C-notes to tear in half and a cool line of patter and a pinky-ring. A *pinky* — Maybe *that's* what she was writing: not "pink" — *pinky*: she just didn't have time finish the word. That little wave of his, too, when that doe came up the steps. Not a friend of his, she didn't acknowledge him, just sat down with some people turned out to be her own crowd. A woman about LaBelle's age. It could've been a signal.

I really want to tell Joey this. But he's sitting right next to Brown, who is starting to put the car in gear. I'm trying to think of something quick and clever, only not so clever that Joey won't pick up on it. We got private signs between us for this and that, for things that come up a lot and that we worked up in advance, but this thing now is a little outside the usual categories. 'Play-Close-Attention-to-*This*-Guy' (two fingers crooked a certain way) could be confusing, since obviously we're *already* paying him close attention; it's the *assumptions behind* the attention that need to change. "Watch-Out-He's-About-to-Make-his-Play" (the right wrist flipped clockwise) isn't quite right either, since I don't know that he is, he's probably just got us pegged for a couple of con artists who hang around cafés. So with the guy now looking straight ahead as the car starts to move forward, and Joey giving me a last glance, I pull a lower eyelid down so that the pink shows, and show the underside of the tongue and crook a pinky, hoping his prior rebus experience from the puzzles at the back of the comic books will stand him in good stead. For now though, he just gives me his You-Gross-Me-Out-Murphy face-curl, and off they go.

I walk real slow towards my rendezvous with death (I always think of it like that, anytime I go anywhere new; livens up the day, plus it's basically true), and my thoughts are churning gears. For at last, and at last, I know something that somebody else doesn't know. But just what? Well, for starters, he doesn't know that LaBelle is dead, or he wouldn't have showed. That's not hard to believe, there's been nothing in the paper, police must be keeping it under wraps while they study the voodoo angle and what-all else I left for them to chew on. Nothing past that first terse bulletin on the police band.

"Cut bait", says his message. It seems early for that, but after all she was only a tenuous possible lead, to Richie; they maybe got better leads now.

Another thing he doesn't know is that I'm *on to him*. Better yet — he thinks *he's* on to *me*. I don't know what his game is, but I know he's a player.

All right now. To the door.

I walk slowly up the long and narrow street, which seems to narrow further as I go. For there is no-one, no-one; deserted since the beginning of time. I stop and listen: alone, with nobody but the wind. I look at the high walls around me and they're not even vandalized, any graffiti long since flaked away. It's like — I stop: feeling shaky. It's like being all alone on a beach, some beach you never been to, only — you've been there, you've been here, in your dreams, or in another life, or just last week but you have amnesia. This dead end, this empty air-pocket in what used to be, in better days, the wrong part of town. And which now is the left lane of nowhere, only reckoned to lie within the city limits by convention of topography. No-one walks these sidewalks, no-one sweeps these streets — which yet are littered with losing racetrack stubs, unsent mash notes, candy-wrappers from discontinued candies, blown in from some other continent. The wind whistles down the main drag westways, and then the earth tilts and it whistles back on the other tack. It is like the long and stretching sands, back when the sun stared down with red-blind Cyclops eye on the primitive landscape, before we even evolved, before the first baffled-stranded fish crawled up (gasping) out of the sea.

And I am swaying here, I could disappear, the sea would creep up and all would vanish. I turn, and turn, searching for some sign that anyone has ever been here. And up a ways, on the other side, a single sheet of newspaper blows: now rising, now sinking and sighing, and rising again. Could this be a clue? But it won't be yesterday's: some other town perhaps, in some other language from some other century, minus a headline, minus a by-line, just been blowing around and around this old earth, up in the jet stream, for years and years, and now settling down here.

A sudden anxiety, like a heart attack. *I have got to make contact, got to see what it says.* I run, I chase the paper, it blows on before, mocking as I lunge and it ever and again, by inches, evades my grasp.

At last I corner it, grab it with both hands, spread it out and scan it as though deciphering runes. The type's

all faded, I can barely make it out. It says — I think —
They're talking about a *man*; there was ... a *person*, and
something happened, something that should not have
happened, that should never have happened,
something very bad; but nobody's sure. Reading
reading, trying to find the text behind the figures on the
faded printed page, to read between the lines, to solve
the cryptogram. But the runes blink back at me, blank
as the sky.

I throw it aside in disgust and look up at the sky
and it's grey, always grey here, no particular season or
time of day; this is where you wind up if, for some
reason, they find your soul too blah and uninteresting
to bother condemning it to Hell.

I whirl around, there is no-one to scream to. North
- South - Left - Right. Why did I come here? How long
has it been?

Got to get out of this, soldier on somehow, I have a
mission, I am here on a mission, if only I knew what it
was. I have got, I have *got* to just reach - that- door ....

I cross the street, wading through molasses. Facing
the building like a mirror — a blind mirror with no
image in it. I lift the plywood, fingers feeling its sweet
real texture. And I am so glad to be here, feeling that
sweet deep wood against my fingers, so glad I am
almost weeping, as it — creaking, lifting — actually
makes a moan.

Dark beyond it. Black, black; stark, dark. Go to it —
Murphy or whatever your name is. That is the path that
you have to travel. That is the row that you have to hoe.

I walk it haltingly, arms out front, feeling the way,
like a blind man, and of course I am blind. I walk for
the longest time, gently stumbling in the dark, and then
come up with a bump, against — something. And I feel
it, feelingly feel it, all over with my happy hands,
running them lovingly over the rich infinite textures,
stone, crumbled, like stucco; and *this* — this could even
be brick! most beloved brick! O God how I love it, this
beautiful brick — its sharp hard chips, as my hands
begin to bleed. I love its smell and its sight (had I but
the gift of sight) and love its touch; and someday, I'll
even see it, when vision is miraculously restored; and I
may in admiration say:

My my; so that is what brick looks like;
isn't that fine ... .

And then wood, *God's* wood. I stop, in reverence.
Good wood, just like He made it, with His huge carving
carpenter's hands. I raise my fist, I say good-bye to life,
then I knock four times.

And when the echo dies (rolling silently back down
the empty corridor), I raise again my fist and, just like
he told me to, strike once again.

And then I settle in listening (this might take days).
It is time to be very (like a mouse) very still. There are

what might almost be noises, far off, and then silence, so near; more silence; and then something like sounds.

They come closer, I tense, I'm in my burrow here like some primitive rodent, furiously-furtively with its sharp teeth, looking out for Number One, fretting and, savagely, waiting to evolve. There is a very short slice of forever, and then the wood gives way.

The darkness gives way to shadow, in which a silhouette now looms. The faint, the feebler dark beyond it, is like a black halo around the head.

"What the hell do *you* want," the head says: and my senses spring awake as at a bell.

Suddenly it is all real again, keen and immediate. There is cigar smoke, and human sweat, both stale in these confined spaces, and some muttering in the background, and the feel of a dank breeze issuing from the doorway, warmer than the dead air of the corridor and more moist. I spring into action, unthinking, grab the guy by the collar and hurl him smashing back hurtingly against the wall.

"You better brush up on your Sunday-school manners, there, asshole," I snarl, "when you're talking to *me*. I come here straight from Pinky, and if you think he's mean when *he's* mad, man, you just plain ain't seen *zip*-o yet. Cause y'ain't seen *me*." Grinding my fist in his throat for rhythm and emphasis.

That was a stroke, that; came to me unpremeditated. None of this "Brown" or "Mr. B." That *might* be his regular handle, but it might just as well be a code, meaning: Don't trust these chumps, they're just messenger boys; or even, Ice 'im when he's said his piece. But they must know the guy and they know how he dresses, and 'Pinky' might even be his real nickname; and if not, plausibly his nickname in some allied crowd that these guys could be made to believe in.

The guy's got a gun, I see now in the half-indoor half-light, but the bits of a second he'd spent processing what I said to him was enough to freeze his trigger finger in that limbo where thought sits brooding hen-like on its throne, and action languishes in chains. But me I am somehow all action, being now snapped out of my trance. I am a man possessed, and what possesses me is unknown but remarkable. Something flashes out, a foot or a fist, and he goes down in a heap. I scoop up the gun. "All *right*!" I shout out in a voice that manages to be both loud and just a little bit royally bored. "Front and center, calling all bozos. Doorman just had a fainting spell. Shape up."

Two men step out of the shadows, like it is timed. Both have pistols. The taller one says, evenly, with intensity but without the sloppy arrogance of the late doorman, "And who: the hell: are you."

Question doesn't bother me; bores me, almost. "Magin's the name, Pinky's controller, just flew in from Headquarters. He did all right this time. The target showed. The message is: '*We fish in troubled waters*'; and I might add, it's gonna be a hull-down catch."

Confused expressions. The tall one wavers, but he bites out his words: "What. Target."

"The LeBaron dame, Richie's twist. — He-ey, wait a minute. Just who the hell are *you*?"

He is not used to being challenged like this, in this way, and his world now tilts on its axis. He has to figure that I'm maybe legit, though he can't figure how, and suddenly he's the one on the hot-seat. He's not buying my line, but he's hedging his bets: the downside to backing the wrong horse here could well be lethal. He doesn't know does his partner buy it — a quick glance sidewise shows only a poker face — but he's forced to consider that self-preservation is probably now uppermost in his partner's mind, just as it is now creeping its feelers into his own. His grey cells choke up, his backbone gives a little, and — and that's the ball game.

A plaintive note has crept in. "I'm Hawkeye — C'mon, *Hawkeye*; Louie musta mentioned me."

Louie. Okay, so Pinky is Louie. Note the name. And lo, another name, Hawkeye, a.k.a. Franco, we meet at last. Please ta meecha, Hawkeye old sport. Y'know, you'n me, we got a mutual acquaintance or two, that I am now going to trot out. It's not much, but, hey: Pawn to King 5. "Yeh, in passing, only I pictured you a lot tougher. — But hey that reminds me — You guys got wind of Richie? Our end, we're still striking out on that."

He seems baffled. "No, not at all. Why — what's the latest on your end?"

"Ahhh, still drawing blanks. Me I ain't seen 'im since that time at Willie's WorldWide." A rueful grin. "What a dump!"

He returns the rueful grin. Yeh, he's been there too; and yeh, we're bonding, all right.

Then I gesture towards his standing companion. "Who's the wimp?"

"That's Bimbo, he's new."

Now that I've got their respect and attention, I can afford to loosen up. "Hey there, Bimbo." A bit of a smile. "Just kidding — no offense." *Their fear I have already; now I want their love.*

"Heyya, Magin," he says back, pleased at being treated like almost a human being by this big shot. He looks down at the crumpled form of the doorman. "Boy, you sure busted Ratso one."

I shrug. "Guy cracked wise at me, makes me nervous, y'know? He'll be fine, he wakes up. Exercise'll do him good. — Kee-*rismiss*, don't you guys got any beer?"

Now he really doesn't know where he's at. He still can't quite make me out, but the last thing a cop or a hit man does when he busts in is to ask for a beer. Actually I hadn't even planned it, all this bluffing just made me thirsty, so that I can't feel my own spit.

107

"Yeh yeh, we got some cold ones in back here." And he shows me into an ill-lit back room.

Still not a palace. Low-wattage unshaded bulbs, no furniture apart from some sticks of wood, some supplies up on a rock ledge where it's cool. He hands me a can of Miller's and I fling it against the wall like the worthless swill that it is. "A *beer*," I specify. He reaches into another cooler and hauls out an amber-glass bottle of the local brew, some stuff they still make like from before Prohibition came along and ruined everything and then the big brew businesses flooded in and ruined the rest. Just plain barley, hops, and water — no honey or corn or flavoring or coloring or estrogen or menthol or whatever-all they dump into these things these days. I savor it, upending the glass, and nod my respect. He cocks his head like do I want another one, and I shake my head No. Then he introduces me around to the rest of the gang; they're about seven in all.

"So," I say, refreshed at last. "Executive summary: How far have you guys got so far, on our project?"

Some awkward shifting from leg to leg. "Well that's — need-to-know. Louie should be here soon, he'll fill you in."

I shoot him a glance that would drill steel.

Again, he goes a little weak at the knees. "No look — hey — no offense. It's just, we figured he'd be coming in person. No no don't get me wrong now, you got Louie's signature, only sometimes he just sends some button, and like, usually they're more, like, quiet and polite."

I shake my head like I'm looking at a sorry specimen. "Boy do you got some learning to do."

No answer to that one.

"Louie never mentioned Magin?"

He shakes his head.

"Good, good." I give a secret smile like I'm pleased. "Louie knows how to keep his lip buttoned. I like that in a guy. — But he did tell you about Plan Alpha, right?" Again, a sharp glance. And an answering bafflement. "Well, I'm the guy that sets it going till the relay team cuts in."

"Plan — Alpha? Oh, yeh, right, um, he did say somep'm about that. Only, no details." An expectant look, hoping I'd fill him in.

But all he gets back is a disgusted look. "Well of course no details. Details depend on how your set-up is *right now*. Could go this way, could go that." I narrow my eyes in a faraway way, as if remembering capers past. "Anyhow we couldn't go dotting the eyes and stuff, two weeks ago, in our planning session, back in Marseilles."

It was a gambit. At worst, it couldn't go too far wrong — just one more confusion, town's pretty mobbed-up after all. But this one hit the bull's -eye.

Everyone goes quiet. Hawkeye is the first to speak. "*Marseilles*? You from the head office?"

I scowl at him in mock-disgust. "Hey, how long you been with us, anyway? Don't you know nothin'?"

You know it's amazing, how effective some ludicrous thrust like that can be. Hawkeye by now has killed maybe six, seven people, what I heard; and heisted things, and been in meetings with people would make your blood curdle and your hair curl. But he was once three years old, and was once chewed out by his mom. And maybe, just maybe, before he turned too hard, he was sent down to the principal's office — enough to make any lad's blood run cold. And there's this vein in him, where these anxieties still live, a vein he is not aware of and does not control. And you hit the right tone — you're right into that vein, it's like a root-canal; putty in your hands.

"Three years," he protests, "but I — oh man this is great. The head office! It's ... an honor to meet you. Sir. Finally. At last." His eyes start to sparkle — could those actually be tears?

Coolly, but not unfriendly, I reply: "You know, Hawkeye, this might surprise you, but up there at Headquarters — I heard one or two good things about you too."

So for the rest of the afternoon, he was spreading out what he knew like a stamp collection, trying to impress me.

I chuckled indulgently. "So, what's the highest guy you met so far in our outfit?"

Rather proudly, though deferential in demeanor: "Well, that would be Monsieur Charnu."

I broke into a guffaw. "That twerp? Back in Marseilles, he holds the towels in the john — when we let him, when he's been good."

Hawkeye wavers in place, paleness passing over him in waves. He's never heard such talk, he can't handle it, he is out of his depth entirely. And it is gradually dawning on him that — kills or no kills — you come down to it, he's just a punk-out small-town Jersey hood.

"S'okay, Hawk', I like your style" I say, breezily generous, with the sort of generosity that a Big Man tosses to the peasantry when it costs him nothing.

He brightens, but uncertainly; even my praise makes no real sense. "C'mon siddown, I'll fill in the details of Alpha based on your update — Well, no, I don't even know what to ask and what not. All right look, it'll be simpler you just lay it all out from the beginning, bringing things up to developments so far. Then I'll tell you what we do next."

He told it all eagerly, without further prompting. I didn't have to ask any substantive questions: just sit there, wisely silent, with hooded eyes. It's amazing how you can get a reputation for genius, that way.

It was late April, he said, that they got wind of a rumor that one of the Scabroso connections was going to be setting up freelance and was fishing for offers. No details, no names. But see Louie and the Scabrosos, they are like enemies and friends. So — and upside, or a downside, you play it just right. So some little tiny threadlike feelers went out, and by mid-May a guy who knew a guy what had talked to a guy who got through to a party that ... and before you knew it two *tons* of pure heroin were sailing the lonely seas looking for some kind soul to take them in. And the Morsue people — cause it's pretty much gotta be them, their Stateside branch office — start feeling their udders full of the milk of human kindness and they want to take these orphans in. But the whole deal is extra delicate because the outfit in the middle that was supposed to be moving the stuff, is understandably miffed, and some rat may've tipped off the Coast Guard, though at this point this is the least of our worries. The Morsues stand to make a killing, and maybe to celebrate with some killings as well — they're a high-spirited bunch; but the hang-up is, none of the other guys wants to get killed.

"My my my," I thought to myself. "What a tangled web we weave."

And suddenly, I'm completely happy. This is going to be *fun*.

So, so far so good. Only, one little hitch, which by now is an itch I can't scratch. And that is Louie, a.k.a. Pinky, a.k.a. Mr. Brown, a.k.a. the Angel of Death. Because no way he'll fall for all my nonsense, he's used me like a punk, and the minute he finds out how I've

112

been scamming, death would be the least of what he'd do to me.

Plus what, he's basically got Joey hostage. So I gotta do some quick thinking. Somehow … ambush him, head him off at the pass. They've got a shed out back, maybe I can lure them in there.

But suddenly the path is decided, because the phone rings and it's Louie on the line. Hawkeye answers, says Yes yes, we got the message about the target. And hey, Magin's here, and things are going great.

Magin.

Magin? You know — Marseilles ….

He hangs up and looks over towards me vaguely. I don't even leave him time to let a thought form in his mind.

"Okay," businesslike, biting off the words, "I was afraid it might come to this. Hawk? I can count on you, right? Yes; yes I know I can count on you. I'll be back in the shed; want to see Pinky in private. Got that? Tell him to come alone." I've come to realize that "Pinky", although understood, is a less-than-respectful nickname, and I need it now. "You send him to me, soon's he arrives. The rest of you — just sit tight."

"Is there … a problem, Mr. Marseilles?"

Grimly. "I truly hope not. But he just might be getting a little big for his britches. There's been some talk along those lines, back at Corporate, back at the Island."

Dark is falling. I head out to the shed. Turns out, actually, almost a barn — some reason, there's hay-bales here and there. So I take off my jacket and take off my hat, and — why stand on ceremony — take my trousers off too, and stuff them full of hay, like a scarecrow, which I seat at the back of the barn in the half-light, a piece of pipe crossed in the arms like a shotgun. Then I climb up into the rafters to watch the fun.

The minutes pass, each one like a century; but before too long, the doors burst open, and Pinky — that rat, I *told* him come alone — Pinky and a grey companion flash in; Pinky with a sidearm, his trusty sidekick with a Tommy-gun. And without waiting to hear my perfectly reasonable explanation, they blast the figure to tatters, the air filling with straw and smoke.

I consider what to do. Kill them? No; I'm not a killer. (Although an oily voice inside me says: Why not try it? It might be fun ....) But definitely take them off the chessboard. So from my perch, I hit Pinky behind both knees, and he goes down. The other guy I don't know him, I'll give him the benefit of the doubt. I simply drop down from the rafters straight on top of him, knocking him flat. The Thompson, I yank out the magazine and fling it into the dark. Pinky I cold-cock — had enough of his chat. The other guy, I prod him awake with my toe.

He is roused, and he rises; but only so far. I haven't so far said anything, but, seeing my .45 trained straight on his face, he remains on his knees.

And so we stay there — me standing, him half-standing, in silence; while the fading light filters in weakly from the dusty panes high, high up on the walls. Slowly the shadows creep over us. I don't say anything, because I have no idea, no idea at all what to say.

I have the leisure to look at him. Grey, close-cropped hair. Hard hands — trigger-finger probably callused to a fare-thee-well. A body not all that powerful, but what does he care, he's got an equalizer, and more than an equalizer, because usually he's got the drop. Grim lips sliced by a diagonal scar, could almost be a dueling scar, from another time and place entirely. Still he kneels, breath heaving, but otherwise not moving.

It is getting dark; it is getting darker. And still I do not know what to do.

And him? Slowly he rounds his shoulders, and slowly he joins his hands — as though begging me for his life; and yet not; he doesn't say anything, or even look at me; he's begging something else, of someone else. I just stare, not knowing what to say.

Finally he pipes up, voice rough like a file: "Just — *do it*, dammit: do it. What are you waiting for? It was you, down here, it was me, up there — you'd be dead by now, I'd be smelling the gun smoke, filling my lungs.

Just pull the damn trigger, what's your problem Jack, you got a hangnail or something? Just do it; just pull it. Asking no questions, for conscience' sake. I'd do you in a heartbeat — done guys like you, so many times it slips my mind. I done 'em at dusk, and I done 'em at dawn. So just do it."

I lift the gun a little, and I wave it aside a little — it is lighter than a feather, in my hand.

"Just ... *do it*! Doncha see?" His voice getting wilder now, though his head still stubbornly bowed. "Every minute I live, every second I go on longer, I'm just digging that much deeper my own personal hole to Hell. I got hatred inside me, like acid in a vat. Like a scorpion stewing in its own venom. If I can't sting something — *damn* you! — it curdles in my tail and makes me ill. It were me — I'd'a killed ya, and ripped out your arms, and sucked out your guts, till the pain goes away. And I gotta keep doin' it, and doin' it, and doin' it, cause there's this guy that I just gotta pay."

I shrug vaguely, stalling for time. "Yeh well. We all gotta pay down our debts."

And now he looks up, he's beseeching me. "But not — not **this one**. I'd do anything — anything — not to pay on *this one*. Shoot me full of holes, shoot me full of lead — blast me, burn me, blow me away — till there is nothing left, nothing left to collect on. Reduce me to dust and sow it broadcast in the fields of weeds. Without memory, without tombstone. Do it now and do it fast, do it hard and dark and dirty, gotta make things right, it's the only way, cause what I done, — I should never have been born. I'm a curse on the Earth. My mother, better she would of died in childbirth — heck, my grandmother should've been strangled in the cradle, and *her* mother and *her* grandmother should've been swallowed up when the earth gave way — all the way on back to the beginning of things, to that — *Eve* dame; she should never of opened her legs to Adam. It all went downhill from there.

"So shoot me now, shoot me clean and deep. Cause I'm a thief, and a killer, and a coward, and a liar; and the singing of swift bullets is the only song I know how to go out on."

I scratch my head and screw up my eyes, "Heck I believe you — you'll do lots more bad stuff. Maybe for days, maybe for months, maybe for years. I tremble for our banks and our virgins. But hey. If the Grace Train ever pulls up, whistle tooting, outside your window: Get on board, brother, just get on board."

So I knock him to sleep with the butt of the gun, keep him quiet for a while, then I toss the gun aside and walk away out into the vacant lot where the sun is gone and yet in memory sizzling singing, and the sky bends backwards like a snow globe over us tiny little snowman figures, making strange gestures, and trapped in the glass.

Chapter Six

I walk slowly back to the clubhouse. Interestingly, none of the gang has come out to see what is up. Seems surprising, but — Why get shot? Why get involved? And who is the top dog you take orders from — Pinky or Magin? It is all so confusing. Best to keep your head down, and wait till the smoke clears.

I push open the door. All is silence, and expectation. No-one is holding a gun.

They've had no idea at all, who would walk in. Me, alone; or Pinky, alone. Or me, with Pinky on a leash.

I wave them hello, and with a nod that says, At your ease.

Silence for a while. Then from the back of the room, someone shyly speaks up. "We ... thought we heard gunfire ... Sir."

Grim-faced, I nod, leveling with the troops. "It was the Scabrosos. They double-crossed us. It was a set-up, a hit. I barely escaped with my life. But Louie ... ah ... may he rest in peace ...." I bow my head, and all do likewise.

The commemoration over, another voice pipes up. "Sir ... There is something you might do, for Louie. Before he went out there, he turned over a prisoner. A stoolie — maybe the bum that tipped of the Scabrosos! We were gonna fix 'im but — maybe you would like to do the honors. In honor of Louie's memory."

Very solemn, like an undertaker, I say: "Show me to the prisoner."

They take me to a far-back room. It is dark. They turn on a lamp. It is light. And there, manacled and gagged, sits ... Joey. And I realize that, when they say "fix", they are not talking about "fixing him up for life", by, say, contributing to his retirement plan. "Fix": as in, *wagon*; not as in, *ticket*. The deal is, they want to retire him right now.

And this I cannot permit, though we both were to die defying it. Very bad things happen to my normally pleasant personality, when I suspicion that anybody is planning or plotting to harm one single hair upon my brother's head, even if it's a hair he's not using. I mean — he's like a *brother* to me, you get me?

So I do two things. First, I resist the natural temptation to free him from his bonds and scamper out of there. We'd get about two feet. Second, I cry, arms thrown out wide: "Giuseppe! You! In America!" And I kiss him madly on both cheeks. "Paisano! Paisano mio!" This naturally stuns everyone, and hopefully stuns Joey enough so that, when I pull off the gag, he doesn't immediately blurt out "O Murphy! Pinky is wise to us! We should never of come here!" or like that. So I'm slapping him on the back and doing this sort of Corsican yodeling, and motioning for the others to take off the cuffs.

Joey, unfortunately, doesn't catch on real quick. "What's with this 'Jew Seppy' business, Mur —

phphphphphphph ...." and I'm laughing and slapping
him on the back he starts coughing and almost to puke.
"Giuseppe, of course!" I cry. "You ask yourself, how do I
know your new code-name? You naturally think back to
those by-gone days when I knew you as Joseph, and
you knew me as Magin. But you — you have risen; and I
have risen too! Now they know you as Giuseppe; and
me, your old friend Magin — back at headquarters in
the south of France" — bending down and lowering my
voice —" (that's on the Mediterranean, there, Joey,
that's this like ocean, just so you know)" laughing and
slapping, slapping and laughing, —" and now, they
know me as: Marseilles!"

At first everyone's astonished, but then some of
them just give up, and start chuckling too, at this great
funny joke.

Now, some of you might maybe be wondering, how
one fast-talking guy could work his way in like that. In
a nutshell: I just give 'em more than they can hope to
process; then they're putty in my hands.

See, the human brain, lemme tellya bout it, case
you don't know. Me I know all about it, read it in the
papers, plus talking with this guy in a bar. Anyway, the
brain, the human brain here — thing you gotta
understand is, it's just ... not that big. It's just this little
jacked-up wrapped-up fatty thing like you'd turn up
your nose if you saw it at the butcher's, and this thing
gotta fit right inside of your skull, plus leaving room for

like the eyeballs and miscellaneous mush that I don't
know what the heck it's for. Just a buncha gunk to stick
Latin names on. And most of it, the actual brain part, it
don't even think, most the time, it's just like the
animals got. You got a sniff department, you got a slurp
department, and a sex department, and like that. Just a
tiny bit left over to try to actually figure stuff out.

So see this brain thing, it's made outa meat, just
like your basic bologna, or your sausages, or — anyway,
it's basically meat, but you can think of it as more like a
lot of little switches and stuff, just like in your car, the
plugs and points and the spark-plug wires. Lots and
lots of little tiny connections, there must be hundreds
of 'em, but the point is — *there's still just only so many.*
And half of them's already permanently occupied
thinking about food and sex. Some guys, more'n half.
So any time you got a new idea thrown at you, it's these
leftover little overworked think-switches gotta handle
it. And maybe they're tired, the idea comes along and
gets 'em up outa bed. So the man's tense. An'en, you
come along and hit 'im with a *nother* new idea, and it's
like, whoa there, the man is up against it. An'en you
keep doing that, another and *another* bait and switch,
and pretty soon he don't know he's coming from he's
going, he's like one a these waiters with the dishes all
stacked up along their arms right up to the shoulder,
just teetering. So the man is all loaded up, every circuit
busy, every relay tied up, warning lights blinking red,
alarm bells ready to go off, an'en, — he makes a bad

mistake. He sneezes, or he tries to chew gum, same time as doing all that other stuff. And he blows a brain-gasket. If you could lift the lid off his skull, you'd see steam pouring out, just like from a radiator.

So anyhow, I got 'em eating out of my hands. And then suddenly — keep 'em off balance — I can the comedy and get all grave.

"Let us have a brief communal prayer for the soul of our dear friend Louie." Who is actually still alive, waiting to wake up with the worst hangover of his life, but hey, a moment of silence never hurt anybody. Anyway, everybody bows his head. "Lord, good old Louie, he was one of a kind. Don't make 'em like that nowadays. They done lost the machine parts to even do it. A discontinued model. Anyhow, Louie done some bad things, but maybe he'll do some good things now, if he ever gets the chance. Anyhow, bye now, thanks God, and — keep in touch. A-men — eh, men?"

And amazingly this is like the best thing ever happened to any of them, nothing like what they've known before.

Hawkeye speaks up. Usually these guys just cuss, but he seems really moved. "I — didn't know him real well, but I took his orders. I only saw him once; he was a goodly hood."

"Amen to that. He was a man, take him for all in all. We shall not look upon his like again.

"Aye, brother, a man's a man, for all that. But — Magin — what do we do now?"

"Now we adapt to circumstances, like the fish in the sea. We carry out: Plan B!"

"And ... what is that?"

"That's where I take his place, and run the show. The crime must go on!"

Then they break into a cheer, they hoist me up on their shoulders. I tut-tut them down with immense modesty, and say they're a bunch of great guys, and you know what, I'm gonna knight them, that's right, gonna turn 'em all into knights. So they kneel down, and I wield a beer-bottle like a scepter, and touch each one of them once on either shoulder. And in chorus, each one, kneeling, doing obeisance, chimes out: "Lord — I am thy liege!"

Joey and I retire alone into a back room, myself giving the faithful a backwards lordly wave adieu.

Once inside, Joey looks at me in astonishment. "Jeez, Murphy, when did *you* get charisma."

I smirk; I got a lot right now to be self-satisfied about.

But he fails to sign up for my fan-club. "Murphy — the idea was to *investigate* organized crime, not to *organize* crime. What were you thinking?"

A bit miffed; a bit defensive. "Hey, it just happened. I just got a knack."

But Joey ain't buying it. "Question is, where does it come from, this knack?"

"*Come* from? Whaddaya talkin'ere? Comes from my big brass balls."

Joey considers. "There's that; but now it's more than that."

And when he says that, something clutches, like an indigestion.

Joey eyes me keenly. "You done your homework for today?"

"What, my — look, Joey, we been busy, obviously!"

"Homework time, Murphy. No dessert till ya done your homework."

"No but — *Joe*- eyyyy ...."

He says nothing.

I bite my lip and then I start. "Heil ... Heil ...."

"*Hail*, Murphy."

"Hail ... Murphy ... — *full of piss 'n' vinegar*!" I roar, or someone roars; and all at once I know he's right and I am sick at heart and I know I just come darn close to blowing everything.

What passed over the next half hour is not to be retold, any more than the tales of the Confessional. When I came out of it, I was drenched in a cold sweat — the same kind of sweat that erupts when at last a fever breaks and leaves you. Anyway, the homework was done.

When I emerged and Joey saw me, he nodded approvingly. "You done the right thing, Murphy. At some risk to your life."

"Better this life than the next one," I said.

And then, something funny. Something really simple, you might think. I need to go out and take a piss.

They don't got a john in this little clapboard hideout; so I go out into the night, beneath the stars.

And I walk a ways out, somewhere near the shed; and then zip open my fly, and just let it flow, it's like — zip and nap, just a little little nap, and —

— *closing round my throat — hard hard — no breath — the windpipe — but for survival — I am swirling around, and punching, pounding — slashing, smashing, and something's slashing back, it has a knife, and it is needling around my throat, tickle-tickle — but I blast it back, and it goes in, right back in to the throat that meets the chest that meets the arm that has the hand that holds ... or which held ... (as it drops to the ground) ... the knife.*

Exhausted — plus my trousers wet, the least of my worries — I wrench the head up by its hank of hair ... and it is Louie. I'd hoped I'd cold-cocked him, must've struck him just a glancing blow.

I drag his body back to the shed. I close the door. I do what needs to be done: slipping his pinky-ring off his cold dead hand, since it might come in handy some time. Plus a couple of other items that he has no further use for. And then, exiting once again into the cool night air ... I notice that my fly is undone, and make the necessary adjustments.

Ready for business.

I smooth back my hair.

Walking on ... A dead man ... Been quite a night ... Got to deal with this-all later, because right now ....

"Hey, Magin!" a voice rings out.

"Yeh hi, 'ts Okay, just been out here takin' a pee ...."

Around nine of the clock, the truck shows up; dusk has come and gone. It's a semi, and it's a beauty. Big wheels in the moonlight, in the admiring glow of a fat full moon. There are no streetlights around here, but the boys play their flashes over it like running their hands over silk. This baby's going to be their ticket to riches.

Doesn't look like a drug truck, just to look at it. Got this big picture of a grinning crumb snatcher with a topknot, kind of a carrot-top topknot, plastered big and bold on its side, with a kind of quizzical smile (or, considering more closely, perhaps just a tad demented) tipped and topped with a glinting drop of drool on the lower lip. And then in big letters:

SCAMPERS
and
Softie for Baby — Safety for You.

There's just one guy driving it, no-one else in the cab. And he pays me no mind because, what does he know. Everything's jake.

Okay, now for the fun and the games.

I stand, legs planted apart, staring off into the middle distance, hands clasped behind my greatcoat (which I managed to cop from a storeroom), in the middle of a field. My men stand reverently about me. "All right men; full battle rattle ; we're going into action. Line up."

They do, just like in reform school; only eagerly, without resentment. I review the troops.

Joey is watching me closely, see that I don't fall back into my Mussolini thing; but this time it's in fun, and he can see me stifling down a smile.

Of the guys that're still alive, we got Hawkeye, the Doorman, the driver, and two guys, Oily and Timmy, about the same size, unidentical twins; plus two other guys that (years later, memory fading, as I write this down) that I can't rightly remember their names — anyhow both end in -o. So all right. The Murphy Brothers, plus the Seven Dwarfs.

"I don't have to tell you," I tell them, "that Plan B calls for the utmost dedication; and, not incidentally, an immediate disbursement, to each one of you, upon successful completion, of a very significant portion of the loot."

A murmuring; a suppressed hurrah. I mean, really — does it get any better than this?

"In addition to the drugs themselves, of a value beyond calculation, there will be a box containing packets of expertly, freshly laundered American currency, in nice delightful small bills. And in twenty-four hours, you are all going to be very, very rich men."

They're grinning and nudging, they're adjusting their eye-patches, *Gawd* it's fun to be pirates; they are (each, gigglingly) digging my speech.

"We are all in this together, men!" — heck, I could go on like this for hours, maybe figure out some way to work-in "O Captain, My Captain", or the Gettysburg Address, what I memorized (a ruler on the fingers, by way of mnemonics, back there in the correctional home); but Joey is giving me the nudging elbow plus this Put-a-Lid-on-it-Murphy (like) look. So I wrap things up.

"Now before we hit the beaches, men — we are going to cement our sacred comradeship with ..." (I kind of choke up here) "with ..." (each expectantly, leaning forward) "with ... the *Napoleonic Oath* !!!"

They gasp; hand flies to mouth; they have no idea what I am talking about, but, —

Good God, it's good ... ...

"Present: side arms."

Each one of them — some of them close to weeping — offers up his weapon; offers up his life.

"Now get in a circle."

Some sobbing now, they shuffle into one.

"Now raise your right hand, or your left hand, whichever one you shoot with. Link arms ... and kiss the pistol of the man next to you."

Some of them blush, and some of them almost die doing it: but they do it. Some of them probably falling fainting; others, getting hard. Electricity is crackling 'round the loop.

"And now we chant ... the Gangland Anthem. I'll sing it first; then you join in."

Well, I made up the words on the spot; these they just came to me. To the tune of "A Hundred Bottles of Beer on the Wall" (me'n Joey — one of our favorite songs). And I do hope that these lyrics came to me from a good place; but if they came from a bad place — What know I? I am but a man ....

One for one, and *all* for all,
and *every*-one for the *gaa*-aaang ...!
Some will rise, and *some* will fall,
and *some* will have to *haa*-ang !!

They join in heartily, lustily, stomping around and like, whooping it up.

And then someone — crazily, but hey — strikes up "Sixteen Men on a Dead Man's Chest"; and these guys what ain't sung, most of them, since they been in kindergarten (that proverbial mean nun whackin'em with a ruler, they don't sing — *Sing the Little White Duck, you miniature miserable sinner*!), the rest take it up, lustily, lungs exulting and expanding, yo-he-ho-ing, here in the dust of the urban badlands, in the stifling smog of the wastescape, in the forgotten Nothingness of this — *vacantlot, downonyerluck, themsthebreaks, takewhatitakes* — — beer-bottles (glaive-like) waving aloft, full-throated showing, no audience but the gulls. Then finally I say (perspiring; imagining pray-ers without words):

"All right men; fall out."

And they are like : *loving it*. Loving it! It is like — summer camp (what they never known), only with guns....

All right guys: *show time* ....

They get their gear together, all flushed and eager. One of them says to the Doorman, "How come Louie never did neat stuff like this?" "Yeh, this is terrific," says another. "Let's go kill someone."

"I'm up with the driver," I say, waving as I climb into the cab. "The rest of you pile on in back. Giuseppe, you come up on the cab with me."

"No no!" they shout. — Uh-oh. What is this, already a mutiny? I raise my hand but they're all revved up — not resenting Joey, but: wanting a piece of him. That blasted celebrity-by-contact dynamic again. You can't

131

fight it. — I shrug acquiescence as the little guy, Timmy, climbs in next to me in the cab.

"Giuseppe comes with us!" cries Oily. "You been over there, right — at Headquarters?" "Yeh!" shout the others, "tell us about France.

And again: Uh-oh.

Cause see — *me*. I get interested in things. I read up about 'em. I hit the flicks, know all about places like Casablanca and Paris and Marseilles. But Joey, see, he's mainly a comic-book man. He mostly knows about places like Duckburg and Metropolis — made-up stuff. And I'm worrying he's gonna maybe put his foot in it.

Now, me? I put my foot in it all the time, I just keep dancing and nobody notices. But Joey — I don't know. Someone will ask about the Eiffel Tower and he'll say, Uh-h-h, couldja spell it? Because even your random hobo knows a thing or two about France — heck, some of 'em fetched up on a beach in Marseilles, got laid there and tattooed there, back in the day; some of them even fought there, like I did, back in the war; but Joey's younger and he missed that action. Doesn't really know France, from a hole in his pants.

So — inspiration — I call out to him: "Hey, Giuseppe, *merde, bon appétit! Escargots apéritif voulez-vous-couchez-avec-moi!* Only, just don't tell 'em about *Slobovia*, okay?"

And while Joey is trying to process this, one of them cuts in, "Hey, you been to *Slobovia*?!" And another says, "Hey, where's that?" and —"Oh hey, yeh,

I heard of it, Near Russia." "Hey you know I think my grandfather came from that place!" says a guy that probably never even knew his dad. — And so it goes, cherubs watching sadly from the lips of clouds: as, with a whoop and a holler, they hustle my Joey bodily up the ramp to the back of the truck.

I wave. Brother's gonna be all right.

The driver grinds his gears and we're going. I'm sitting in the middle, Timmy on my right.

"So," I say, making conversation. "Whadda y'all plan on doing with your share of the loot?"

Hunched over the wheel, Oily. His eyes are glistening. He's barely begun to speak, and his voice is already hoarse.

"Ho boy, *me* — I'm gonna buy me a broad an' I'm gonna *stuff* 'er; an'en I'm gonna go get drunk an'en I'm gonna *stuff anudder one*; an'en I'm gonna go get me some *smack* and get *smashed*, an' some *crack* and get *crashed* —" and all the while he's thumping the wheel, and pumping the gas, in time with the words; and the truck is just lurching along.

Hard to know what to say to such a thing. "And ... uh ... pizza?" I venture. "Cos you'll have the munchies after all that."

"Ye-e-eh-EH-eh ... a *pizza*; a *big* one, wid' *everything on it* — wit' — *spit* on it; *come* on it; **blood** on it; d-d-*duck*butter ...."

"Ahhhhh ... Ho-kay. Think I'll stick wit' anchovies. — And how about you, Timmy? Whacha gonna do with *your* share?"

He looks doubtful. "Gee ... I don't know. How much you figure it'll be?"

I say to him evenly — no sense being a piker about this: "I reckon it'll come to a coo-ooll quarter of a million." Doing my Bogart bit; imaginary cigarette dangling from the corner of my seen-it-all mouth.

Silence; gaping; something happening, in his head. "A quarter of a — ? Holy — ! — ... *Jeez*, I had no idear!" — It's like a bomb fell on him; he's just blown away. "*Jeez*, with a quarter of a — jee-eez, I mean — wi' money like that, — - ... ... : **I : could : go : straight** ... ... **!!!**"

I stare at him, not believing my ears.

"*Jeez* ... wi' money like that, I could, I could get mar-ried! For real! A nice, swell girl! We could — we could have a : *family.* An' oh — oh — jeepers, oh — cripes, we could have a, like, a little like, *real house.* In a *town.* With a *fence.* A white ... fence ...." The sweet sob that is rising in his voice — I am just frozen; I could die right now. "Yes! An' like — some kina *yard*, wi' like — *grass*, 'n' like ...." He's sniffling now, I don't think he ever even seen any stuff like that but in a magazine. "Oh, I could — put up, *swings*, for the kids, the lit-tle **ti** — ny — kids, — — *oh* please, O please, *O* ... let it be ...." He's put his head down on the dashboard, and he's just weeping.

Oh God; oh God. The *way - you - made* us. Scratch any one of us, deep enough, scratch past the crap and the crust and the dried-on vomit from last night's drunk: and we want to be one of the good guys. And we mostly don't even know it. And instead — a slip here, a wrong turn there — and we spend all our time, a stranger to light, just barfing around in the dark among the garbage cans.

Chapter Seven

A dock, south of the city. Hasn't been used in years. Seen better days; then seen worse ones; then seen others that just plumb sucked ....

A fog's rolled in, and dusk is dropping. Out over the water, just a faint hint of a moon. No breeze, nothing stirs; the silence. Nothing for it now but the waiting. Wanting won't hurry it up.

The way I piece this thing together — and I can't ask too many questions since supposedly I already know — is that what's coming in, is a legitimate ship, in a sense; got papers for legal cargo it's going to drop off a little later, no problem with the Coast Guard at that point. But right now, they got this other cargo too, traveling steerage as you might say; and that's what we come for. Cause a shipment this big, and junk this pure, you don't want to trust it to the little dodgem boys and the luck of the waves. You want delivery, and no hitch. There's some funny connections been made, and both the usual plus some unusual people been paid, and we don't want no runners getting caught and start blabbing, and stuff being traced.

So we're lying low, truck parked a good ways back from the docks. Lights out. Radio silence. Nobody around for miles. Just cornfields — was once; only now, no corn. The last time this place seen its salad days, Coolidge was President, or one of those guys.

Every couple of minutes or so, Hawkeye works the blinker light: real quick, tap tap tap, flashing a signal out to sea. A brief, hopeless-seeming signal, to the immensity of that dark. Then we strain our eyes and not seeing anything but just straining them keeps our senses keen; and so we do hear, the little waves of the silent mid-tide lapping, close to the piles. Shh shh ... hush ... The dark is really closing in.

We are sitting in darkness. Some guys are smoking, little lit tips like fireflies. Somebody's cracking his knuckles. Oily's got a little penlight, and he's carefully going over a girlie mag, tit by tit.

Hawkeye blinks his flash again — more times than necessary, he is getting impatient, all this silence and the dark — and this time a light from offshore answers him, a complicated pattern, very quick. A murmur of approval ripples among the guys. Hawkeye turns to me and says, "What'd'ey say?"

Say hanh?

"C'mon, what'd'ey *say*."

Say? They said like: Blinkblink; blinkblink blinkblink; blinketyblinkblinkblink; ... What, ya want I write it out for you in Braille ????

"Dammit — *you* know Frogtalk: What - Did - They - SAY ???!"

Uhhh ... "Who. Me? You talkinaMe ???"

"YEH I'm talkina You. Louie was supposed to decode it, but now you're in charge, so like, do your *job*."

And before I can answer, another set of syncopated blinks, very, very rapid. I don't know Morse Code and anyway this is probably Morse for some other language, either plain Finishing-School Frog, or else something they set up special, just for this job.

Well, like my Pappy woulda useta say (or so I suppose): Don't sweat it. Just wing it. So I do.

"They *say*," I say, squinting, "All agents ... at the ready. Place lamp ... at end of dock ... to guide us in. Maintain silence." I mean, it sounds reasonable. (I resist the temptation to go on, "Have you heard the one ... about the hoodlum and the Frenchman ... who walk into a bar ....")

"That's *it*? The whole message? All those blinks?"

"Yeh well, the first part was just the usual French politesses, hard to translate. And towards the end they switched to a different, close-hold cryptosystem, known only to the top dogs up at Headquarters. But what the heck, yeh, I'll tell you what it said. It said: Drive the truck ... down to the docks. Kill the engine."

"Kill the engine?"

"Yeh, that's what they said, kill the engine. Probably gonna take a while to load."

Again their eyes go greedy at the thought of the richness of the coming plunder.

So Hawkeye's acting like foreman now, and he says, "All right men, you heard 'im. Let's move it on out."

They do move. You can almost smell the greed, the sweat, and the saliva. Hunking on down through the darkness, like trolls in the mines, wheeling out the dollies, breaking out the burlap, getting it all set up. Waiting for our ship to come in.

And slowly, slowly, it does so. Just looming up out of the fog. First you can just make out its prow, then a widening wedge of the bow; it's like a ghost ship coming out of an iceberg, all the lights are off. And then finally sliding on out, like a long cigar.

They cut the engines and just drift the rest of the way in; then they briefly rev them up again in reverse and quickly cut them again. And now they are motionless, just a couple of feet from shore. Some ropes appear in the air, cast from a high rail; we tie them to cleats, and then wait.

I sort of go "hooo", long and low, in case it's a signal; and if it isn't a signal, well, what the hell, I can go "hooo" if I want to.

For a minute, the ship just sits there. Dark and silent. Perhaps it really is crewless — perhaps it just floated in from a century ago — perhaps it is cursed. We gaze up, necks cricked, as though some ghostly figure would appear on deck, raising a ghastly skeletal finger and — And then, silent but for the creaking of joints, they lower the gangplank. You can't even see the guys doing it, they must be in blackface and wearing black, it's like the ship itself is doing it: and it somehow gives me a chill like a .45 in my mug never managed to do. Still it sits, while the minutes tick. I can actually sense the goose-bumps of the man next to me. No-one dares say a thing; and still, not a soul, not so much as a shadow has appeared on deck.

And for a minute I'm thinking: Maybe I'm not the smart guy; maybe I'm the dumb guy after all. Because maybe, in about six seconds, a flash of badges and drawn weapons and shouts of "*Freeze!*" will come pouring down the gangplank, leaping over the guardrails, and I'm back down on Murphy's Luck: busted.

Or: Maybe I'm *half*-smart; just unlucky. It's not the Feds, it's the Mob all right, but a different Mob, not our Mob, and they swarm out and kill us and jack the truck and sell the stuff themselves, cutting out — rubbing out the middleman. It'd make perfect sense. All kinds of disasters would make perfect sense.

Like, even — as the seconds tick (tick tick) (TICK TICK!) by, and my eyes get wilder ... Maybe it's — *aliens*; and they haven't come to buy anything, and they haven't brought us anything to sell. It's *us* they want, gonna place us in slavery, working over in Sicily, as monkeys for the guinea grinders, iron rings round our necks and chains on our ankles, dressed in little red jackets and no pants, bowing and scraping at dockside tables in Corsica, maybe, the chain firmly anchored at the base of some pissoir, to keep us from jumping into the ocean and ending it all. Being used for female purposes, dog-fashion, in the bilge of tramp steamers and the backs of trucks, by unmannerly mouth-breathing profusely-sweating truckers and sailors. Being forced to lick their tattoos. Swabbing the decks with our tongues.

(Horrible; but it gives me a hard-on.)

But then a door opens somewhere up there, it appears like, cause there's this blue glow. And then a slim single figure in a sea cap and turtleneck, outlined against it, appears at the top of the gangplank with folded arms. Our flashlights throw the shadows of his elbows and shoulders back against the walls of the wheelhouse, like sable wings.

Dead silence. Nobody moving, neither down here nor up there. For a crazy quick moment, I am tempted to surrender, to throw myself upon the mercy of that stern still figure, silent and high. And yet I know, in some sane place of me I know, that that mariner-prince, that prince of mariners, that prince among princes of the lords of men, knows no mercy. Blandishments, yes, and come-ons; but of mercy, not at all.

So instead I revert to the Old Murphy, just crazy-old, plain-old, magic-dancing Murphy, who knows not what he is doing but who does it just the same, trusting in Whoever guides his flapping footsteps, unseen. "Hey Pee-air, moan-a-me, gladja could make it!"

142

The figure startles, loses some of its brooding presence, then says, "Lou-ee?"

"Nah well, Louie coulden make it," I say, and I start up the gangplank. "I'm handling it now."

"Very slooey," he says (sounds like), glaring at me, not even bothering to go for his gun.

"Very slooey to you too. Where's the drugs?" I picked up a few French greetings back when I was over there in uniform, but this one's new to me.

Then he says it louder, like he's angry, although I suspect that it is something slightly different than that; and all I once I tumble to he wants to know *where Louie is.*

"Oh yeh, Louie, good old Louie, he, hey, *you* know, this 'n' that, stuff comes up — he hadda see-a fella bout-a dawg." By now I've reached the top of the gangplank, and suddenly about fifteen spotlights come on Zang! and I'm the star of the show.

As the Feds like to say, I "freeze". It seems much the wisest thing to do.

Guys with rifles, in sea-kit so similar it might as well be uniforms, appear lined up all along the edge of the deck, all aiming towards the same place as picked out by the spotlights, namely me. I get a feeling of that funny freaky-flesh, you know how you feel when your little brother or your sister is approaching your ribs meaningfully with an extended finger, not yet actually tickling you but broadcasting unmistakable Imminent

143

Tickle intent, and you cry out "Mo-om ...!" but the dang kid hasn't yet touched you, (tickle tickle) technically not yet touched you; and technically you can't bust'm; — anyhow, feels (achingly) something like that. Little tiny bull's-eyes on my pale soft skin, where the bullets would go: exploring me first with their snub little noses, before sighing and sinking deliciously in.

And so it goes, the confrontation: Murphy the 'Murrrican; and these silent guys from across the sea. You can tell as how they're foreigners, cause nobody had of clued them in on that, in America, when you come to America, you like, smile, big smile, big friendly smile, alla time smile. But: These guys: Not smiling. The way they're looking is — must be some kind of French thing — it's like: We do not know you; We do not wish to know you; and if you should crook your leee-tle, very tiny pinky, — we fucking plug you, *un point c'est tout.*

Now see, it was *us*, going over *there*, we'd a been slapping backs and grinning and passing out sticks of gum. And saying, Which way to the Awful Tower so's we can save it from the Nasties? And marrying their cousins and showing them photos of our sisters and singing folksongs in their cabarets and kissing the barmaids behind the hayricks and conceiving little lisping semi-Frenchmen and going back to Iowa and forgetting all about it but maybe, say your daughter's born on July the 14th, maybe naming her Suzanne Marie instead of Susan Mary like you'd planned, because that's how Americans are — big hearts, big balls; brains, sometimes not so big, but good people you get to the bottom of it. But these foreigners — well, it just goes to show.

And then I figure: What the heck. You live scared, you die scared, right? Tons of guns trained on my own some, but who cares; doesn't take but one of them to kill you, and you could just as easy die crossing the street to go to Mass, some runaway pie-truck and you're a grease stain on the road. So I turn to my men and wave them on: saying, in the totally convincing tones of sheer fearlessness — not the same thing as actual bravery — because indeed I am without fear, being (a) stupid, and (b) on a roll, and (c) in the bosom of Abraham, or so it would appear: "'T's'alright, men, everything's jake, I recognize some of these guys, knocked back many a *vin ordinaire* with them, back in the day, c'mon up, they won't hurcha, they're with us." And I break into our campfire song. Hawkeyes starts up the gangplank and the rest follow, singing along.

The guards train their rifles on the moving mass, but now they're wavering, not really aiming, they're not sure. For there is something about song, bellowed forth by the masses in motion, which doubles and trebles the vastness of the mass. That is why the Bastille fell, back there, back in the day, way back in France.

Plus, there's the logical considerations. After all, they were expecting to be met, and sure enough they have been met, at the right place and the right time.

145

The sable trim guy seems to have qualms, but the crew, they don't know Louie from Adam, or me from Eve. Really the only hitch so far is the jaundiced eyeball on the French officer, who personally I've got pegged for a royal bastard, and he probably treats his underlings like dirt as well. Plus as I keep coming closer, it gets to looking like most of the sailors aren't even French. Oh, they're from the shores of the Mediterranean, all right, but not the Cote d'Azur, more like Sardinia to Albania to Lebanon — the Phoenicians, back in the day — and then down around those funky shady places along the southern rim, the Barbary Coast. The type of guys the Marines had to go in and set to rights, like in the Hymn — the Shores of Tripoli. Not a striped shirt, not a beret in the bunch. No, push comes to shove, these guys don't owe no loyalty to some stuck-up, jumped-up little Parisian prick.

Plus what, come right down to it, our guys marching fearlessly forward got Tommy guns and sawed-offs and flame-throwers; and one of 'em, swear-to-God, just got a big wooden club with a spike through it, somehow more threatening than anything else. So now the guards on the ship start to kind of act casual, inspecting dust-spots on their cuffs, scanning the sky for kites, whistling little melodies remembered from the Old Country, kind of chilling things out.

Me and Hawkeye get up with the French fellow, whose face — unlike the blackness of his cloak — is now a ghastly white; and I give him my most friendliest grin. And then — pressing my luck, but hey, like old Casey Stengel says ... — I give him one great bit sloppy smacking European kiss on each cheek; and beam at him like he just done real good, done his duty on the potty.

The hatred in his eyes would chill my blood, in normal times; but these aren't normal times. "Stop it - Right - There," he says, with as much menace as he can muster.

The whole thing is going over just dandy with my men; even the guards on the ship are observing some leadership which, while absolutely off-the-wall and loony, does manage to compare favorably with the Captain-Blight scenario of their own vessel. It's like — American-crazy versus Frenchman-sane. Take the former any day. Anyway the officer is staring daggers at me, but he doesn't move, I mean what can he do, he's just been punked right in front of all his men. Men who each come from their own particular village, back in the scrublands or the Rif, and who were scraped together for this one job, and paid wages of some ridiculous pittance, and who owe this bastard on the fo'c'sle no loyalty at all.

And then I deal him a rabbit-punch. "So hey, Pierre, you've got a problem of some kind. You might consult a shrink. But in the meantime, kindly allow me to see the captain, if it wouldn't trouble you too much."

Now, this works either way. Either, (One), *he's* the captain, and I just innocently mistook him for the hired help. Or else (Two), he's not the captain, so I get to go and see a different guy, who cannot possibly be worse than this one.

Really, it's amazing, how the balance of power can shift so quickly, and on such a small scale — like a bubble in a spirit-level. Be it the Bastille, or Boston Harbor, or the Winter Palace: most earth-turning Revolutions have involved just a handful of guys. Guys in the right place, at the wrong-right crazy-mixed-up time. And with the right brass-balls attitude.

And turns out it's Two, looks like, because he gives a sharp nod, like you can almost hear his neck click. Like he's saying to himself, That is *just* who you're gonna see.

Oh, well, okay, you got an even bigger badass back there in the cabin? 'K, bring'im on. I'm in it *this* far.

Now — lemme step back a bit. Because — *you*: here you are, you're reading my case files; and you're skeptical. No no no: I can tell, I can tell that you're skeptical. You are saying to yourself, "Christ, this cannot be *happening*! Murphy, you are out of your *depth*!"

Guilty on all counts. I been way out of my depth, since the day I was born. — That day, only single thing I knew, only sense I was born with, was: The Tit; Find the Tit; Seek It Out. Which is great, only ... Never did find it. Damn bitch forked me over to Foster Care and blew town — the Fosters, what fed me on 'formula', some sort of rank vomit they stick in a bottle and then shove down your throat and I spit it right back up. But I drank it; had to, eventually, that or die; yeh, I drank it; beggars can't be — can't be *jack*, Jake. — It's like — me? I die right now? right here? this very spot? Last words are:

Mothers, feed your babies, if it's the last thing you do;

do it do it do it, though you die trying, better you should die right now, in rivulets of blood and milk, than fifty years later, covered in diadems and diamonds and shit and spit and sin. Just like the Man said, the Man on the Mount: *Feed — My — Sheep*. **Feed** my ... *effing* ... ... **bleeding** ... ... *sheep* ....

He shouts: "Eh, Red!", and pretty soon this beefy type appears, that the only thing's red on him is his piggy eyes.

"Please ta meecha, Red baby," I say. "You the captain?"

"First mate."

"So ... why am I talkin' ta *you*?"

"Count of I speak English, what the captain don't not."

"'K, sounds like you speak American, same as me. Anyway, Louie couldn't make it, scheduling conflict, and I come to close the deal."

He scowls at me, and his bulk fills the field of vision. "I'm dealing with Louie."

"You're dealing with *this* —" and I hold up Louie's pinky ring right in his face. "The Sign of the Sapphire. DOOM to him who disobeys!"

Now, that's flaky and a half; but I figure, a smuggler's life is pretty cut-off and screwed-around anyway, all lies and disguises, so that their sense of reality must get a bit bent, and maybe he'll buy it.

He buys it. Shrinks back. "Wherejoo get that? You bump Louie off?"

"Not him," pipes up Hawkeye, referencing me with his thumb. "The Scabrosos. We had a hit."

Oh the Scabrosos, huh? We'll see about that. They're messing with the wrong mob."

Uh-oh, what've we started. Oh, well.

The first mate turns around and bellows, "Eh, Cappy Ten!"

Cappy Ten shows up, looking trim and nautical like a captain should. After all, he'll be dealing with Customs a little later on, once this part of the cargo is gone.

I look over at Red like a question.

"Go ahead. He doesn't speak it, but he understands."

"Hiya, Cap'n. I come to close the drug deal, the one that Louie was running. See, old Louie got taken from us, he has gone to another world, and now I'm in charge."

150

His eyes, as pale and grey as the sea, are as unfathomable — you can't really read them. He says quietly: "Name?"

"Oh hey, that's real good, you speak real good English, there, Cap'n, swell how about that, you parlay just great."

Again, on the same tone: "Name?"

"Name? Who, me? Yeh, ah, the name thing, right, it's, ahh ...."

Hawkeye breaks in. "His name's Magin, but they call him Marseilles, count of he's so high up in the Riviera mob."

I want to step on his foot but it's too late.

"Ah, reelay?" he says to Hawkeye, and then he turns to me and says something rapid and fluent in frog talk. I mean, I guess it's frog talk. Maybe Corsican, for all I know; or Sardinian, or Sicilian. Anyhow no hablo.

Bad news. Fact is, about the only word of frog I know for sure is "merde", and I'm wondering how to work that into the conversation — like, maybe try to distract him, point and say "Hey, Cap'n, I notice you got a little ... *merde* on your gaiters there, like we say in Paris." But then I remember this great shtick I heard once on the radio, a husband-wife team, and the whole thing consists of just her saying "John", and him saying "Mary", but the different ways they say it as the thing develops, it's like a whole romance, from soup to nuts. So I try it, sort of heaving my shoulders with a Gallic shrug, and then I say: "Merde."

My guys grin and nudge each other in the ribs. They're loving this. That Magin! He sure is one swift linguist!

The captain seems less impressed; he says some more frog-talk, this time more slowly, as though spoon-feeding a foreigner.

I throw back my head and laugh like I get the joke, and shout, "Merde!" and then "*Merde* merde mer-dy-merdemerede, m-m-m-m-*merde*."

And now he gets a gun out, and points it at my belly button, what right now is an outie but it could become a serious innie at any moment; which is sign language in any language, and I start sweating and shifting and sort of babbling, "MERDE merdemerdemerde, me-me-merde, mer-dee-mer-dee-merde ...." Somehow it worked fine on the radio, but it isn't really working for me now.

All right, show-time. You wanna play sign language? Time to reach back to the old ingrained dyed-in-the-wool reflexes inherited from our eons in the jungle. My eyes go big as pizzas and my jaw drops as I stare and point behind him, shrieking like a freaking banshee in an unspeakable, ear-grieving, spit-curdling, bowel-loosening hideous horror of terror, "*LOOK OUT BEHIND YOU* !!!" Not like: Sir, there seems to be an ornery cowpoke behind you who wishes you ill, perhaps you might wish to turn around and demand to know his business; no. Rather: Whatever thing of slime and violence you have ever most feared from the deep-down, angst-ridden, fungus-musty strata of your psyche — *that* thing is right now engulfing your head in its hideous maw.

Now, logically of course, he could easily deduce that this red-alert is probably bogus; and with a steady gun-hand and a curl of the lip, delegate to some subordinate the job of inspecting the hinterland for threats; and doubtless, intellectually, he quickly reaches this same conclusion. But when a knee jerks, it does not request prior permission from the thinking brain. My scream connects directly to some deep-buried structure down past where the grey-matter gives out and the reptilian hindbrain begins: for a fraction of a second he wavers, half-turns; and that split-second is enough. I drop him with a punt to the privates and grab the gun.

See, it's a lot like poker. I'm actually not half-bad at that, though it seems that Lady Luck deals me more than my statistical share of bad hands. Because the lousier the cards, the craftier and more inspired is my bluffing. So I usually break even or a little better.

"*So!*" I shout, baring my teeth and pointing the gun at his head, for the benefit of all present. "You figured you could muscle in on us, eh? Thought you could take our money and then shoot us, keep the drugs for yourself and then sell 'em — and then leave your own crew in the lurch and make off with the loot on your own some! — That's what he was hinting at in French, guys, between the lines. — We-ll, buster, I was warned about you in Marseilles!"

His own crew, perturbed, is beginning to murmur; heads nod, expressions grim. Meanwhile the captain is not making any debating points back because he is down on the deck clutching his future generations in his hands, which are about to die like dominoes right down the line, thus bringing his own dynasty, that dates back to maybe William the Clueless, to an abrupt and inglorious end.

"You low-life dago, where'd *you* learn to speak French?" I snarl. You might of at least brushed up your accent. And that anchor tattoo, you Eytie fool, it's a dead giveaway."

My companions crane their necks, and, sure enough, there's an anchor tattoo! — A dead giveaway, they agree with one another and nod.

"Hawkeye," I say, my voice returning to a deadly calm. "Refresh my memory. What exactly is it that we do, with traitors?"

"We plug 'em, Marseilles."

"Right, Hawkeye; as a rule. But you know what the quality of mercy ain't not? *Strained*, that's what." And with that I cold-cock the captain with the butt of the gun.

"Come on, men," I call, "let's get a move-on. This guy's with the rival Chacal gang, and his buddies may show up at any moment to try to take this stuff off our hands."

If you stop to think about it, this doesn't really make a lot of sense. But that's the great thing about the strenuous life. Nobody's sicklied over with the pale cast of thought. No one's "Do I dare?" need wait upon "I would", like some alley-cat in the cabbage. Just keep things moving right along.

They hop right to it, and pretty soon they're carrying the crates of goods down the gangplank like army ants.

"Just load it straight into the back of the truck," I tell them, clipboard in hand. "I'll be there checking it against the manifest."

And I check it, just being curious, because I really have no idea about this deal. Most of the boxes turn out to be full of a white powder. Probably not talcum, coming all this way, but the only way I could tell is to try it out on a diaper rash and I ain't got one, and no baby is handy. Two of them instead contain a big tin, used to hold fruitcake, with now in it a thick brown goo. Really looks gross but what the heck, I'll keep it. Might come in handy to grease the axles or something. Then in the last box, a different kind of grease, sweet and green — palm-oil, the grease of deals.

I'd just been making it up about there being a money-box for immediate distribution, back when I promised the men their dividends, since the whole idea was that cash goes *that* way and the drugs come *this* way; but now that I think of it, it does make sense. Whoever scraped together the big bucks for all this probably paid with hot cash, and part of what he bought is this small-bills untraceable stuff. It doesn't look like much, compared with what the rest of the cargo is worth, but I reckon it's like the little wooden spoon you get with the tub of ice-cream. Just a practical little add-on or lagniappe, to pay the incidentals of distributing the dope.

Which could come to a pretty penny, come to think of it. I start counting it up.

Forty thousand, fifty thousand, fifty-five ... Good thing I got counting down, before bombing out of arithmetic class ... Seventy-five, eighty ... and not even halfway to the bottom of the box. Yes, quite a haul. Only, pretty soon now, time to say good-bye to the haulers.

Joey pokes his nose in and whispers heatedly.

"Murphy, this has gone far enough. What's got into you? Leave that trash aside. They'll be back in a minute and our goose will be cooked, but now they're all down at the ship. Let's just run."

"Aww, Joey, and leave all this neat stuff? Plus my legs is tired, all that stomping we done. Let's just get in the cab and drive."

"Hey, you crazy? You think they won't hear the engine, see us move? We'd be sitting ducks. You know you can't lay rubber with these big semis. They'd plug us in a heart-beat — then no more heart-beats. And hey look, I think I see a couple of them coming up our way now."

I'm back to quickly counting — hunnert, hunnert ten ... Almost half there, and not enough to split it nine ways, not with what I led them to expect. ... — But hey! That's it. <<There should be more>>; the deal was, there should be more.

I quick stow the moneybox. Hawkeye and a couple of heavies are coming towards the truck. I'm sitting in a pool of light around a gas lamp, shaking my head. The box is safely out of sight.

"Big problems, Hawkeye. Call the men."

He whistles, and they hurry up the hill.

"Bad news, fellows," I say, adopting my General-Patton stance. "The drugs is all here, all present and accounted for; but there was supposed to be six millions big ones in small bills."

They gape, they goggle; any critical faculties they may once have had, lie now in smoking ruins.

"Six million, for immediate distribution among us, in equal shares! In fact, me and Giuseppe here have agreed to forego our own portion — nobleness obliges, y'know — so the six million gets parceled out among the seven of you. — Hmm, I don't envy the guy that's gonna have to do the math. — Anyways: Those crumbs on the boat are holding out on us — either that, or someone pulled a fast one back in France. Either way, I am seriously pissed. So you guys go back to the ship and go down in the hold and search everything — everything — understand me? It's *your* money and *you* have a right to it."

Joey's giving me the sour eyeball — that's the kind of blandishment the Dark Prince is ace at, maybe picked up a touch of it back awhile ago when an unclean spirit got temporarily mixed in with my innards. But the men are just loving it. They jump, they yowl, they are up for blood.

"But no rough stuff less'n they talk back. — All right, snap to it. Timmy, you stay here and guard the truck." I don't want the kid to get hurt in what might turn out to be a brawl or worse, down in the dank and the dark of the ship. "And men — as for myself, it is time for me to make my farewells."

They startle; they are all eyes and all ears.

"Men ... it has been an honor to lead you and to serve with you. This day will be inscribed in silver ink, in the parchment annals of crime. As for a share of the take, I crave none, and gratefully leave it all to all of you. — Oh no, fear not, I shall be amply rewarded as soon as I get back to headquarters in Marseilles. A small skiff awaits me offshore, to take me to the Company ship, lying at anchor, off in the fog. We ask Poseidon for calm seas, as we slowly make our way back home. But we cast our fate upon the waves in any case. Farewell! for I must leave you now. Brave brigands — proud pirates — Farewell!"

They get really choked up at this; since for them, life is basically a movie that isn't as good as the movies, and here I am making this great speech. Mostly, their life-movie has been as extras that get greased in the early scenes. And now they're like the Knights of the Round Table, or Robin Hood's merry men. They clap me on the back and they say it's been great, and be sure to write; and they wish me a safe Atlantic crossing. I nod, speechless now, holding back a tear, and with a single, final wave of the hand, I stride tragically off into the dark.

At that point, they snap out of their trance. Someone gives the cry, "Let's go get the loot!" Then with a whoop and a holler they go hurtling down the hill, waving their submachine guns like cutlasses.

When they are out of earshot, we creep back. Timmy is planted there, standing sentinel, alone at his post, accepting whatever Fate hands him, gazing out into space, and up at the stars. I'm starting to feel bad about bamboozling him. The rest of 'em is just mugs could use a lesson, but this kid seems to have a streak in him somewheres, of the right stuff.

And I'm thinking, and it's gnawing at me, and then I got it. I approach the truck. Timmy whirls around and cries "Who goes there?!", clutching his gun. I step calmly into the lamplight, and say, "Hiya Timmy, just forgot my glasses, they're up in the truck somewhere, back in the back." He nods and goes back to watching the stars and I go in and shut the doors and get out the cashbox. And I'm feverishly counting the rest of the cash.

... two hunnert forty-nine thousand; two hunnert forty-nine thousand five hundred; ... nine hunnert ...

159

and ninety-five …. What the *heck*? $249,995 — what kind of figure is *that*?

I'm starting to sweat; time is getting short. "*Hey Joey —*" hoarse whisper —"*you got fi' dolla'* ?"

He swings around — stares at the vastness of cash right in front of us, and my curious request. "Whoa, Murphy, people been laid out cold for askin' that."

"It's only till Tuesday."

"For a hamburger today? No, I know you. *Which* particular Tuesday did you have in mind? — And don't tell me you're gonna pay me back outa *that* there, cause we ain't takin' none of it."

"No no brother, I'm with you there. *None* of it! C'mon, we don't got all night."

"Okay, okay. That we do not." He seems a little surprised that I gave up so easily, not even demanding a teee-nee little wee portion of the loot; but what the heck, he'll lend me a fiver, even a tenner if that's what it takes. Only it has been a while since we been paid. He's fishing around in his various pockets. "Nope; sorry, Murphy. Just two bucks."

"Fork it."

He does. And me I'm slapping my pockets, checking my socks, yeh hey, crumpled-up One in one of 'em, for an emergency, well this is an emergency, that's three, need two more — damn, two bits but no bills, another quarter, some dimes, a coupon, a ticket stub — ah the heck with it, no time to count it now. I'm just dumping out my pockets and stuffing stuff into the box. Must come to five dollars or darn close. I scribble a note and stick it in an envelope. It says:

Buy that house you were talking about, the one with the white picket fence. The kind with a wife in it, raising the rugrats. God bless.

Then I scrawl SECRET PLANS on the envelope, in red crayon, tape it to the package, and rush out and hand it to Timmy.

"Timmy," I say, as solemnly as I can, though my chest is heaving. "You're a man I can trust. You have one more mission before you may rest.

"Take this package personally to Logansport, Indiana, get there in any way you can. Proceed to the corner of State Street and Main. A man in a hat should approach you at the stroke of noon. His face will be devoid of meaning. You will hand him the package, and depart.

"And if, by any off-chance, he should fail to show, it means the operation's blown. Canceled, for all time. In that case, lights out — go back to your home town, to your parents if you have any, to the girl you knew in high school, or wherever you are called. At that point, the package is yours."

He sighs. He's looking doubtfully at the package but he does as he is told, tucking it under his arm. He starts off — and then turns around, and says, "Sir? Uh ... you remember uh, you were sayin' ... we was each of us gonna get a little share? I mean, I don't care about the six million, but ... but it's been a long day, and a short life, and it's just ... maybe just a couple of twenties, for grubstake, to tide me over the next stretch?" He waits, passive and impassive, for whatever Fate shall deal out.

My gaze is steely. "When — and only when — you have completed your mission."

He sighs again. Not a bitter sigh, just ... one of life's sighs. "H-*O*-kay ...." Life has always been like that for him.

He walks off, fading out into the night. I never been to Logansport but I figure, little place like that, they'll have a church or a courthouse or a school at the main corner, and maybe a brunette at a lunch-counter, in a white apron and a pale blue dress; something to give Timmy there the right idea.

To judge by the racket rolling up from down at the dock, it sounds like things are getting pretty hot down there in the hold. The first mate won't much like these guys messing with his legitimate cargo, which is his cover for the whole trip; and my guys won't feature finding nothing but frogs-legs or lederhosen or whatever it is they're shipping over here. So there will be a dispute. Words will be exchanged. Integrities may be questioned; reputations, needlessly impugned. Actual ancestry, possibly, called into question; or a man's preferences in the sphere of Venus, placed in an unfavorable light. Trigger-fingers may begin to itch; and at some final provocation, be scratched.

"Let's roll, Joey. They can't hear the truck start up over all that din, and they couldn't get off the ship and hustle up here in time even if they did."

He puts it in gear and we roll out slowly, sighing and quiet, like a whale getting out of bed after a big drunk.

Chapter Eight

When I wake up, it's dawn, and we're out in the rolling country, not a building in sight. Must've dozed off there. Jeez, it's exhausting, being a crime boss.

"Where we headed, Joey?"

"Just out. You got any ideas?"

I put my chin down on my chest. "I'll think of one." And I doze off.

I come to, and the sun's a little higher, but still it's just countryside. We roll along. Hardly a car on the road.

"Where are we?"

"Not sure. Even-number Interstate. A different state from where we came from, I'll tell ya that."

"You don't think those boys back there might go whimpering to the state police we took their truck?"

"No; but whoever *they* took it off of might."

I look over my shoulder. The coast is clear.

"Hey Murphy, you think you can maybe take the wheel now? I'm all in."

"What, you been driving all night?"

"Yeh, you betcha. We're not gonna stop till we put about six states between us and there."

He means it. We don't even pull over, he just scoots to the side while I hold on to the wheel and arc over him. Now I'm driving, and in six seconds, he's sound asleep.

I feel pretty good here, as Murphy good goes — not even a hangover, count of no booze. Feels okay having this baby to play with. I wonder what this sucker will do?

I floor it, and not much happens, except on the tachometer. Got to remember this isn't a car, it's a diesel vehicle, narrow power range. I must've already been driving it at the top of that gear.

So I shift one up, and it responds nicely, nicely. Thing must have a supercharger on it. Let's try another one. Go-ing UP ....

And so it goes, through the last of the fourteen forward gears. The truck isn't hauling hardly any weight, so it really travels. The speedometer's broke but I'd estimate a hundred, maybe more.

Joey's still sleeping like a baby.

Then I notice we got company. A squad car, pulled up even with us. No lights flashing, no siren; just, the cop on the passenger side, face no expression, nods, and crooks his forefinger, pointing to the side of the road.

And I'm sorry, really real sorry, but this is just not on the program. Not with four tons of smack in the back, and a truck that's not registered in either of our names, what's been stolen anyway, twice over — at *least* twice, who knows how many times this baby has quickly changed hands. Plus the dirt on my shirt, and the blood on my hands ... No, that deal is not going down.

So I nod back, expressionless likewise, and I crook my forefinger, pointing now to the *other* side of the road.

For a moment, I just let this sink in, since it's interesting to watch. Cop's face is beginning to tremble into some sort of expression, only he does not as yet know what kind of expression it ought by rights to be. Fear? Wrath? Puzzlement? Disgust? Indignation? Maybe panic? Or what thoughts ought to go with that expression.

Right now, his whole life is maybe passing before his eyes. Or maybe he's simply thinking: Shit, another out-of-state trucker with attitude. Or it might be, thinking back to that morning's briefing by the chief, when he'd not yet had his coffee and had not yet had his donut — his very first donut of the day — when the chief had said, This 'n' That, Blah de Blah, and, don't forget next Friday, and Miller report to such and so, and Good job whoever, and Bad job somebody else, and don't forget to turn in your such and such to the departmental secretary, oh and by the way, be on the lookout for a stolen semi packed with four tons of heroin and who knows what-all else, drivers armed and considered dangerous, on no account approach this vehicle without substantial backup or else losing your badges is the least of your worries — had the Captain said something like that? It was hard to remember. Yet here was this face, this impassive mask behind another mask of half-reflecting glass, performing a mysterious gesture, echoing mine, almost as though he were my image in a mirror, myself staring back at me, with my cop authority, but higher up in the cab, his spectral cop authority somehow trumping my own. A sad and eerie image, and not the one you would like to have, as the very last thing that you see in this life. As compared with your wife bending over you (and now he thinks of his wife), or your kids clustered round you (now he pictures his kids — Jimmy, Janey, plus the little towhead) or even a priest at your bedside (and now he fervently, fervently, wishes for a priest).

So I nod, and I point, and now a little sad smile; a sad smile of farewell, wishing it didn't have to be this way. Then I just gently turn the wheel, nice 'n' easy, real slow, so as not to break anything, and slowly squeeze them on over to the other shoulder, ni-i-ice 'n' easy ... slowing us down some so they don't get too hurt, and then gently gently tip 'em over into a ditch.

Hope they're not harmed or nothing. Oh well, they're insured.

So I'm rolling along, singing my song, and no bullets whiz after us, and I'm thinking: I wonder if they're hurt.

It can't have been too bad a crash, it happened like almost in slow motion, and the rearview mirror showed no smoke and no flame. — So I'm drivin' and jivin', alive 'n' connivin' ; and then the thought again crawls up on me: Shit — what if they're hurt.

I look nervously in the rearview, but of course by now they're out of sight. Still no smoke curling into the sky. So how might they be doing? Okay, right, I tipped 'em over, shouldena done that, I'm like sorry, okay? I'll contribute another fifty bucks next time they call about the Policeman's Ball. You happy now? Heck, I was slowing us both down, we couldn't've been pulling more than forty when it happened ... could we? Of course, this speedometer is broken, and I'm just estimating, and intense things were happening so I maybe was not estimating all that well; plus just maybe, my memory here is playing tricks on me, not wanting to admit ... to admit ... what I ... maybe ... might of done ....

I see a sign, it says "Gas" plus an arrow, and I take the turnoff. We could use some anyway. I jump out of the cab, attendant's filling us up, and I go use the phone, shoving a shopper aside to get at it. And I shove in my dime, and wait an un-be-*lieve*-able number of seconds till it rings at the station; then I'm talking to the state police, so fast they have to slow me down. I them them I seen an accident, out on the Interstate, and I describe to them the stretch of road. And I say: *Hurry.* — Then I jump back in the cab and we light out of there quick as that mother will light. Joey feels the jostle and wakes up.

"Whadawe stop for, there, Murphy?" he says, yawning and rubbing the sleep out of his eyes.

"Oh just ... hadda get gas."

"Oh. Yeh. Right. Yes. Okay." And he starts to nod off.

"And ... uh ... plus ...." Is he asleep yet? No; he opens one eye.

Low voice.

"Plus a phone-call."

His eyes pop awake. He turns and looks at me screwy. "What, ya callin' yer bookie, placing bets that we're gonna get away with this thing?"

"N-no, Joey. Fact is, right now, were up to me, I'd be taking out loans and laying odds against it."

He sits up. "Somp'm happen?"

"**No**! No, no ... well you know ... this 'n' that ... I mean ... shit happens, you know?"

"Yeh I *know*. Specially with *you* around. So what happen?"

"We-ell ... You won't get mad at me, willya? I mean, woncha?"

"Murphy I'm already mad, here, okay?! So just spill it."

Nothing for it. So I tell him about me playing road-hog with Smokey Bear, and how I turned ourselves in. Well, myself in. Don't worry. I'll tell them you were asleep.

"O-oh, Murphy," he moans. Now he's studying a map. "Look — Turn west here at the next junction.

Then hang a right. We high-tail it down the county road. Buck us over quick into another state. A whole new state police, we just might make it."

So we do, then we zigzag a little, laying down the fancy moves, ducking and weaving the truck, trying to do unpredictable things. And we're listening in on the police band, but so far, nothing. So we drive along silent, each guy thinking his own thoughts. By and by, Joey speaks up.

"Well, Murphy, admit it. Even for you, this has been a pretty amazing day."

I give a modest shrug, but I'm basking. It really was the work of a master, that business down at the docks.

"I mean, let's see. You got: at least three guys killed, and maybe way more; a couple dozen guys fooled, and out for revenge; you hijacked a truck, heisted about fifty million worth of smack; and you left John Law spinning his wheels in a ditch. So — you happy? You done enough for today? Or maybe got some *other* damn fool crap up your sleeve ...."

I am hurt. I shake my head.

"What — me — Happy? Me, Murphy? With a unforgivin' sin squatting right on my soul like an old toad? No, not happy. No Joey. Not happy at all."

Joey calms down; thinks a bit; says: "You still thinkena bout that, huh, Murph."

"*Thinkena* boudit, **course** I'm *thinkena* boudit. We could buy it at any minute, you'n me, way we're running aroun'." I throw my hands up. "Ho, *ma-an*, I

171

can just see it. Show upita Pearly Gates, it's like a party, everybody all dressed up in party hats, but going in all slow and stately, cameras popping; and me I'm wearing a tux. Then I get to the gate, and the doorman sadly shakes his head, and says:

Look down.

So I do, and my shirt-front is all covered widdis e-*norrrr*-mous blotch of barf ... Plus I'm not wearing pants, and I'm barefoot, and my feet stink ... And I'm pleading with my eyes, but he just shakes his head again, and he says,

Look down further

and I do, down, down, further down, into the furnace mouth, and —

And —

Can't handle it.

Joey frowning down at his knuckles.

"Take it easy, Murph."

We drive until dusk. By then the munchies are coming at us like the living dead.

"We got a sam'ich or somethin', Joey?"

"Sorry Murphy. Just a Twinkies I found in the glove box last night. Wasn't too fresh. But I ate 'em both. Had to stay awake."

"That's alright, Joey."

We drive a while and then we see a sign, "Rosie's Big-Rig Pit — Welcome Roy Rogers of the Road".

"Load a that, Joey. What say we all three of us take on fuel."

Well, we been driving twenty-four hours without letup, put a good thousand miles between us and the trouble, like the crow flies, when he's flying to save his life.

Joey says it's jake with him, so we roll on in to Rosie's, fuel up first with some diesel number one case we gotta high-tail it before the fries arrive. Then we stretch our legs and, boy, do they need stretching. We head on in to the eats part, front all white and silver, diner style. Juke box hits us the minute we walk in, plus every kind of grease-smell and smoke-smell and noise.

"Place is all right."

We hunker down at a booth. The menus here are really helpful, cause they're all speckled with different bits of food like free samples. 'Scuse me, miss, I'll have this thing right here. Can you identify it?"

Man, the things they can do with frozen patties in this place. There's the "Trucker Burger", that's two of 'em with home fries in between. "Billie's Bigburger", that's three with cheese. Right up to the "Eighteen-Wheeler", that's *eighteen* of 'em, all in a stack, with a little piece of pickle at the center of each wheel of meat, for the hubcap.

"Oh, hey, Joey! Everything a man could ask for." I wave over the waitress. "Hey, honey, can a man get pancakes at this hour?"

She points to a sign that says "BREAKFAST SERVED ANY TIME", and says, shifting her gum to the other cheek: "Sa-matta, cancha read?"

That burns me up. "Sa-matta, canchoo *think*? Just cos I have pancakes for *dinner* don't make it *breakfast*. Ya get up at the crack a dawn and have a cheeseburger, that don't make it *lunch*. I mean that's like saying you been to the midnight matinee, you had a nightcap with your brunch."

She shifts the gum back to its original cheek, and with a slightly more slurry voice says, "Just don't get on my case, buster, or you can leave."

People are turning half around on their stools and looking at us. Joey tugs my sleeve.

But it's too late, I got my mojo going. "I mean, just cos you scramble an *egg* don't make it morning, y'know that? Only *God* can make it morning, or maybe the weatherman. That ever occur to you? hanh? hanh? I mean, you can scramble all the God damn, sucky runny farm fresh freakin' *eggs* that you want, till you're pink in the tits; but'*at* don't make it —"

"Murphy, Murphy, cool it, willya?" says Joey just loud enough for me to hear. "We don't want trouble, not tonight. Man we got enough smack in the back a that truck to send up the river for a lo-o-ong time."

Just then this big lug lumbers up. "You, givin', Shir-lou, any, guff?" He's breathing hard. Looks like the guy is sweet on Shir-lou.

And I'm just sorry, I mean I know I ought to just call it a day; but twenty-four of the long ones with no food and no beer, and plus us on the run, and havin' no fun — it's like my temper's been sitting out there in the sun, and some of the skin just flaked off it, and it's raw, real raw. So I stand up and I say, really enunciating really well so that everyone can hear it, and getting right up in his face so he doesn't miss a word: "Which one's Shir-lou? The fat one? Or the dumb one. Or the one with a mug like it's somethin' you send back to the kitchen."

Now see: Me; me and Joey — we can do this stuff with each other. Day gets slow, we're sitting around, and I pipe up and observe that his mother is like *thus*-and-so; and he thinks about that a while and then comes back with the counter-observation that *my* mother is like *thus*-and-such. And I consider the point, weighing the arguments both pro and con, and then remark that, that might very well be so, but see *his* mother is like *such*-and-such. We can do that cos we know each other, plus we had the same mother after all (or would have, she'd stuck around).

But this guy now, he got no sense of humor. Just a basic sense of honor. Plus a little slow on the uptake, and slow on the comeback, the fight'd be over before he could think up a single snappy comeback. So he has learned to trust to his fists and not his wits. And they are trusty. The right one now sends me back into the silverware caddy, and then the left one has me back up on my feet in no-time. Then while the right one is considering what it will do for an encore, Joey, who has been observing the proceedings from a neutral corner, now decides to contribute his two cents. Cause, sure I had it coming, and for sure he'll chew me out later for what I done: but for right now, when it gets down to the wire, he doesn't feature how anybody's gonna use his flesh-and-brother for a punch-up toy, however legitimate his beef might be. So he walks over, nods hello, and he doesn't hit the guy, he just steps up behind him and flips him over, holds him up by his waist, walks outside with him, mumbling apologies to the other diners as he goes, and dumps him upside-down in the garbage bin. Then we both hop back into the truck.

"I manage ta grab some sugar-packets on the way out," I say, as the engine rumbles into life.

So we drive along quiet, snuffing the sugar out of these tiny bags like it was cocaine. Only it doesn't taste right and I check and it's saccharine. Not much nourishment there. I crumple the bags up in disgust and we ride on in silence.

It's dark out now. We're way out in the wilderness. We turn down a logging road. I figure, if it can handle a logging-truck, it can handle a semi. We stop at a turnout and make camp.

"Gee, Murphy, I don't think I even been this far out of the city." He is looking around him in wonderment.

We're in a clearing, pretty high up into evergreen country. The sky is just plastered with stars.

We make up some bedding out of the burlap sacks in the truck. The air's a little cooler than we'd bargained for.

Joey's lying on his back, arms cradling his head. "Boy we really mixed it up this time, Murphy." Looks like he's not gonna chew me out after all. "How we gonna get out of this one?"

"Dunno, Joey. Have to tune in to the next episode. We'll think of something. Fact of the matter, I'm not even that worried about it. Got my mind on something else."

We lie silent awhile, appreciating the evening air. The lack of smog is a little unnerving, but I guess you get used to it after a while.

"Hey Murphy, refresh my memory. Why do we do these things?"

"We're lookin' for Mallow, remember?"

"Oh yeh, Mallow. That's right. I forgot."

We're lying on our makeshift mattresses looking up at the stars, and it's like a tune running through my mind, with no music and no words. After a while I think Joey's asleep, but then he speaks up again.

"Hey Murphy, you sure we want to go on with this? Sounds like Mallow's a wrong guy. I mean, what do we do with him if we did find him? Beat him up?"

"Course we ain't yet heard Mallow's side of the story."

"That we ain't not."

"Two sides to everything."

"Yep — that and a dime."

You stare at one star long enough, it seems to disappear. Your eyes go out of focus, or your mind gets tired. I mean I guess that's the explanation, but what it looks like is, the entire star just ups and disappears.

Just like Mallow. — No, wait, getting my metaphors mixed.

"Hey Murphy —"

"Hey what's with this 'Murphy Murphy' stuff. You want I should go get you a glass of milk?"

I'm ticked off; he interrupted my star.

For a time we just lie there. There are wind sounds, but they sound far off, like the winds in some other heaven. And what might be coyotes, far out in the wilds where it's really really cold, you can barely sense the sounds of them as the wind whispers in and unrolls them like seashells from a wave. Mostly I'm listening to even softer, much nearer noises: a leaf falls, tipping this way and that as it does so; some grass rustles; something brushes against a twig.

Joey's been thinking. "Mikey ... I got to thinking. Us not having a mother, kind of sucked."

"Plus no dad. — Yeh well, that's life; our life. 'You make your own bed and you lie in it', as they say."

"Really! Do they say that?"

"Yep. Just like we're here lyin' in ours right now."

"Yeh ... Pretty decent beds at that. — Ground's kind of stony, for just burlap, though."

"Good for your muscle tone ...."

And then: "Hey ... Mikey?" He says it slyly.

"Yeh, what?" My suspicions are aroused.

"You ever gonna get married?"

"*Me*, a detective, married? A married detective? Who ever heard of that."

"Just askin'."

I'm soaking up the dark like a lotion. It restoreth my pores.

The truck sits in the dark like a gigantic teddy-bear.

Me I'm just lying here, not hardly thinking, it's like my mind is a space-ship, like Flash Gordon has, and we're cruising right out among the stars. Where a soul cannot sin, where there's no temptation. Just God's back yard.

And I'm lying here and I'm living and breathing, just soaring through space. And all the stuff that bugs you, back in the city, the gang wars and cop cars, hard guys and neckties, phone bills and liver pills, it's all washed away. The things you done and seen, it's all just like skin or clothing, shedding off; and the guys that begat the guys that begat the guys, all the way back, climbing back up the generations till it all just vanishes at a single point: you are just the way they were, really. They lived, they bled, they died; but they didn't die, for here you are. And you'll bleed, and be in need, but some day it'll all recede, and you'll be up there with them. And with Him.

You can figure stuff out, on a mountain.

Chapter Nine

We woke up when the woods did. They seemed to have survived the night okay, but we were both stiff and cold and groggy.

"Man I'm hungry, Murphy."

"You can say that again." I looked around and around at the bushes and the rushes and the depths of the trees. Slowly the eyes narrow. "My hunter's instinct is up."

"Same here." It's a guy thing. Inherited through the Y chromosome. "So let's hunt us up a diner."

He didn't have to say it twice. We tossed all our gear in the back of the truck and sped out of there, heading back down to the valley, and not looking back.

Joey summed it up nicely. "Nature's okay to look at, but not to eat or sleep in."

"You got that right. Nice place to visit, but you wouldn't want to live there."

"Plus dangerous, way dangerous place. Might get a tick bite."

"Poison ivy."

"Rattlesnakes."

"Polar bears."

"Yeh, tell me about it. Nature's okay in her *place*: on a *postcard*."

"Yeh!", laughing, "A postcard, saying 'Wish you were here'."

"Yeh. 'Wish *you* were here — better you than me!'"

"Let's head back to the slums, where we have our happy home."

And so we do go, pickin' up mo', just rolling on back down the hill.

I'm driving this time. Joey's looking around, taking in the scenes. Still nobody much else on the road.

"Hey Mike, yawanna just dump the dope? I mean, we're not gonna eat it or deal it."

I rub my chin. Huh, needs a shave.

"Well, true, but let's hang on to it for now. You never know. Modern life is so uncertain, you just never can tell when four thousand pounds of pure uncut heroin might come in handy."

So we roll on, doing duos to pass the time. We do love songs and beer songs, and even "The Little White Duck", which is one of Joey's favorites.

Pretty soon we spot a pickup truck and then another one, and then a big camper going the other way. Then we see a semitrailer and some trucks parked by the side of the road. A little scuffed-up sign reads, "Pecos Biff's". They don't hardly have to advertise — no-one else for miles and miles.

"You-reeka. Eats." We curve on in.

A lanky guy over by the gas pumps smirks at our truck with the baby logo on the side, like it was *us* that was changing the diapers. What — so he's hauling like jockstraps, or pig-iron or something? Jerk. I scowl at him like he better watch his ass or we'll be changing *his*. — Don't linger to press the point, though, since last time we missed our meal that way, and by now our stomachs are beginning to digest their own lining.

We bang on in through the screen door. A few flies bang in with us. Much warmer down here than in the mountains.

Five or six guys hunched over at the lunch-counter. All's we see is their backs, and the logos at the back of their feed-lot caps. [Editorial note: Modern readers will be confused by this. But at the time that these events occurred, now lying in a dimly-remembered past, caps were worn with the visors towards the *front*, as they were designed to be worn. Additionally, at this ancient period, underwear was generally worn *beneath* the outerwear; but such observations would take us too far afield.] No-one turns and waves. No-one bustles up to inquire how many in our party and would we prefer smoking or non-smoking and may we show you to your table. We grab a booth.

"What're y'up for, Murphy? The runny eggs or the burned toast?"

"They can dish out runny toast and burned eggs for all I care by now. I'm so hungry I'd could eat a quiche."

The waitress strains over like we got her out of bed. Actually wouldn't mind getting her into it. It's been a while.

"Gennilmin be having?" she snaps her gum.

We order the "Ranchero". I refuse to actually use the word — I hate it when they give these gay little names to these things, so I just point. And what it is, is, see, it's like you got this flapjack sandwich — see? flapjacks instead of two pieces of burned toast — and then eggs- and -sausage stuffed in between the two griddle-cakes. Maple syrup on top, which makes it sort of hard to just hold it like a regular sandwich, kind of defeats the purpose, really. Tasty, though. — I don't want the waitress to hafta keep popping back while I signal bug-eyed with my mouth full for more coffee, so I ask her to just leave the pot. She shrugs and does.

My kinda place.

I'm hardly half done munching when already I'm up for some culture. I'm just that kind of guy, doesn't live for his pancakes alone. And the great thing is, they got a sort of culture module right at each table. It's this little like individualized selection box they got right at the booth, you put your nickel in here and it feeds into the big pot-bellied job they got, like a country stove, over at the end of the wall. Can you feature it? Jukebox menu, right at your own table! Grandpa never had the option. The march of progress.

So I'm forking with one hand and flipping through the options with the other. Lessee what we got here. Hm. "Birmingham Jail." No. —"Jailhouse Rock". Uh-uh —"Live from Folsom." No way. —"Take a Message to Mary". Dang! —" I Shot the Sheriff." ... This is starting to put me off my feed. And while I'm trying to decide, someone else shoves in a slug and the juke roars to life.

Chuh-boom, chuh-boom. "I-Fought ... the Law-haw and the: **Law Won** ... I-Fought ... the Law-haw and the: *Law Won* ...."

We munch and we chew and we wash it down, but now it's got a rangy taste to it. Joey keeps looking back over his shoulder, and I keep listening for sirens.

We toss some bills on the table, and leave in haste, not waiting for our change.

"Y'know, Mike," said Joey, after the outdoor air had had a chance to freshen our faces and bring us back towards our senses. "I'm thinking we oughta repaint the truck. That crumb-snatcher logo's too conspicuous. If there's an APB out on us with a description — and by now there must be several — that little kid might as well read 'ARREST ME'."

"All's I got is a magic marker. Guess I could sketch a moustache on. He'll still look pretty much like a kid, though."

"No I mean: Have it painted. Painted *over*."

"I dunno. You bring in a truck, obviously a commercial truck, and obviously your employer wants his logo on there. Driver doesn't get to change it just cause he'd rather see something different on the side — like a couple of hamsters, say. — Hey, coupla cute hamsters, might not be a bad idea after all! — No but —

the painter guy might get suspicious, make him antsy, no telling what he might do."

"Well so, we pay 'im so it doesn't bother him anymore. Buy him his peace of mind."

"Now you're talking like me, Joey. Pay him with what? A cup a dope?"

"No, no way, but there was a bunch of money, too, right."

"There was." A pause.

"So, how much was there?"

"Well, the operative word is 'was'."

"Oh, hey, in English."

"See, I give it to Timmy. Kid looked like he needed a break."

"That was nice on ya, Murphy; but now *we* need one. Guy would spot this truck three states away. It's a cinch we can't go back home with it."

"Ye-eh ... Y'know, Joey," I say, stretching. "I was thinkin' of taking a trade-in."

"Who'd trade for this?"

"Oh they will. We'll trade down."

"And where we gonna find the other trucks?"

"Well, right there — there's some beauties right there in the lot."

We pay our tab and mosey out to where the trucks are parked. A sun-tanned guy with a stubble is messing around with a three-axle. It's ... well I can't hardly half describe it: it's nondescript. We stroll up, we say hi he says hi.

"Hey, buddy, howja like to trade trucks."

He shrugs, not even looking around. "Naw."

"We're talking semi, here."

Now he does look around. He squints and takes in one of us, then takes in the other. He looks over at our semi, towards where I'm nicking my head, then looks back at his little van.

"You're crazy. Semi-trailers cost a mint."

"Yeh but, see, we got a special delivery to make, over a hill and across this little bridge, it won't take a big rig."

"Oh, *I* see, you just want to borrow it."

"Yeh, right! That's it: just borrow it. With the semi as collateral. We leave you the semi, we take the van. Plus we'll fork you fifty when we get back."

He's scratching the back of his neck. He's a skeptical man, but turn it any way you please, sounds like an air-tight deal. "Okay. Sounds like pretty good security to me. Is there a catch?"

I shake my head. No catch.

"Well ... oh-*kay*-ay ... Make it sixty, though. The wear and tear."

"Not a problem. Fact, we'll make it seventy, you help us load the diapers over from our truck into yours."

"How long you be gone?"

"Bout an hour."

"Sounds good. — Hey, wait, though. What if you have an accident?"

I give a brief laugh. "Well heck, you're that worried about it, why don't we just sign the semi over to you? and you sign your wheels over to us? That way, we total your vehicle, we die in a ditch, you're covered and then some."

He laughs nervously. "Hard to find a flaw in that — for me. But for you — What's to keep me from just driving off with my new legal semi-trailer and all its papers while you're gone?"

I look him in the eye. "We don't think you'd do that — you have an honest face. But if it puts your mind at ease ... If we're not back here in three, four hours, you can go ahead and do just that."

His eyes go wide and he shakes his head: crazy world. "Boy it's a pleasure to meet a fellow that's so trusting, on the up and up. This day and age."

We make little "aw shucks" motions with our shoulders and our toes.

"C'mon, what're we waiting for? Lemme give you a hand with the goods."

We load it over, each man passing to the next, like a fire brigade. It's not all that heavy, the way it's packed; but there's a lot of it.

" Man, you guys sure do have a lot of diapers."

"Yeh well, babies poop a lot."

The work proceeds in silence. But then a bag breaks and some white powder leaks out.

"Hey, what is this stuff anyway?"

"What, that? Talcum powder."

"Oh yeh, right." He looks back at the painting of the baby grinning goonily down off the side of the truck. "Their little butts."

We close up the tailgate. He hands me the keys and we climb into the cab.

"Say," he calls out, over the sound of the revving engine. "How come you guys gotta *special-delivery* this stuff?"

"Oh well, they got them some real bad diaper-rash back there in the hills. It's like an epidemic."

"Oh. Well — Good luck."

"You too."

So we roll, on our new wheels, in our new world.

"Hey Murphy" says Joey when we've driven a ways. "What's he gonna do when we don't come back?"

"Drive home and show the windfall to his wife."

"You don't think he'll call the cops?"

"Don't think so, Joey. You don't do that to a gift horse. Plus he may start wondering whether what he did was legal. Not sure myself."

"He could phone it in anonymous."

"Cops won't move on that. Switching trucks without a notary? Not that big a deal. Plus it would bounce back on him, since if they catch us, the truck *we* got is signed over from *him*."

"He might not stop to think of that. Didn't seem all that savvy."

189

"Hey anyway, we're covered. Truck is now in our name. — By the way our name is Orson Ferra, anybody asks. An I.D. Louie had on him when he died." I show it to Joey. He curls his lip.

"What — you pick the pocket of a corpse?"

"No no, I was preparing him for a decent burial. Anyhow he doesn't need it now, plus it was phony in the first place."

Joey softens a little. "Oh, ya buried him, huh? That's good. Consecrated ground? Well no there wouldn't be any out at the hideout. But anyway, howja manage it so fast, I mean all that cement and asphalt, and you with no shovel?"

"We just had a simple ceremony. Shoved him under a pile of tires."

We roll most of the day, playing the radio loud. Country-Western, seems right for the longitude.

What with all the driving and diving and looping around, we'd somehow wound up in Nevada. So we check in at a chicken ranch and rented some chickens. Then I bought a cowboy hat, and felt much refreshed.

"Whacha gonna do with that hat, back ina city?" queries Joey. "You'll look ridiculous."

"I already look ridiculous. It'll look great on the moose."

We ease into Reno, and I say: Hey — Like to try our luck at the tables? He says: Whereja get all this money all of a sudden? Back in the truck there, you were down to borrowin' offa *me*."

"Yeh well, then I remembered. Louie, um, had some in his wallet, when he died."

"Aw, you didn't!"

"Hey, the man was up for meeting his Maker! You know that one about the rich man and the camel what walked into a bar? Or something like that. Anyhow, they both got dissed at the gates of heaven! Hey — I was doin'im a favor!"

"Murphy, Murphy," Joey shakes his head. "I don't know what to do about you."

We-ll ... Easy come, easy go, like my Pappy always said (though not to me; never met the man). Coupla hours later (Reno time; might be more than that on a regular clock), it's all gone. I sort of lost track of the time — they keep bringing you free drinks.

"Well, Joey, sorry. They cleaned us out. Not my fault — Lady Luck was on the rag. Guess we'll have to sleep in the truck."

Joey's been playing pinball; not a gambling man.

"Yeh well, that's nice for tonight. How we gonna get gas? How we gonna get back?"

"Shoot, Joey, didn't think of that."

"Well, I *did*," and he flashes a roll of twenties. "Cos I figured you might do this."

"Hey whereja get that, Joey? You been dealin' our powder off the back a the truck?"

191

"Bite your tongue, Murphy, and chew it, and swallow. No — I got it outa your own wallet, same like you done to Louie. That, or you'd a blown it all at craps."

"*Why you* — ! — Oh. Ah. ... Oh ... Well, actually: thanks."

We're walking back to our motel-on-wheels when Joey stops in his tracks.

"Stare real hard at this slot machine, Murphy."

Makes no evident sense, but I do as I'm told; the brother does not waste words.

"Now scratch your cheek and yawn and kind of peep over your shoulder and try to get a good look at the guy by the purple door; but don't let him get a good look at you. Use your shoulder to shield your face."

I do, and he doesn't. It's a guy from the boat. The frog on the gangplank — or whatever he was. Not American, unless he was putting on an act.

"Gotcha," I whisper. "He just went through the door, with a guy in a tux."

"What's he doing out here?"

"Maybe he's on vacation."

"Going through a door marked Private? Must be a working vacation."

"Hm. Maybe something went wrong with his shipment."

"*Maybe*? We only, like, lifted it off them, then left them to fight over some made-up money, with Louie's boys; and that was before they even knew they'd have another disagreement about the drugs."

"Yeh, Hawkeye and his guys won't have a too-easy time of it, when they go to the receivers and say, Sorry, we ain't got the goods; and the enforcer says, What happen to it, it get on its little legs and walk away? and Hawkeye says, No no, it was taken up bodily into Heaven by your good friend Marseilles, just as you presumably ordered him to do. Who come out of thin air and went back into it. — Man, there's gonna be more theories than a physics department. The mystery man is X; he is Y; he doesn't exist, Hawkeye lied. Hawkeye stole it; the boatmen stole it; it never even left the French docks."

"Y'know, Murph, this town just doesn't do it for me. Too high a density of ramblers and gamblers, and of guys that we don't want to meet. Let's move out tonight. Let's move out — now."

"Yeh, heck, you're right at that. Let's just head on home. Can't be any hotter for us there, than it is here."

So we climbed back into the truck, and with a sigh, not looking back, drove out through the desert, in the gathering dark.

***

We rolled home without stopping, spelling each other at the wheel. Finally reached our old office lateish

Friday evening, parked the truck in front. Trudged up the worn old stairs. I opened the door and flicked on the light. It looked like a hurricane hit.

"Jeezers, Joey, we been vandalized!"

"Exactly the way we left it, Murph. You just forgot."

I'm walking around the room with this blechh of disgust. "Then what's this baloney slice doing, hanging from the antler of the moose?"

"You was makin' a samwich, and you got innarruptit."

"An'ese *shoes*, ina *sink*!"

"You was thinkin' a cleaning' 'em, I think."

I stared, incredulous. "You tellin' me, we ... *live* like this?"

Joey shrugged helplessly; but his eyes were gentle. "You know how it is, Murphy: We are fallen men."

I sighed. "Yeh well; anyhow. It's good to be back."

"You got that right, good brother of mine. No place like home."

Chapter Ten

The next day I stepped out to get a newspaper, see what the burg been up to while we were gone. Headline said: GANG WAR ENTERS FIFTH DAY. Same amount of time we been away.

I showed it to Joey, and he started to shake. "See what we done now?"

I shot back: I'm not taking that rap, we had nuttina dowiddit, wasn't ina neighborhood, I was out walkina dog.

"No, look, Murph — it's a cinch it was us got it going. Lookit — six bodies discovered at a 'bandon dock south a the city; Disabled ship, no papers; Rumors of vendetta — it's got Murphy written all over it."

I crouch off grumbling, and go scrounging around for the comics. "Yeh, none a my look-out. Coupla hundred mobsters more or less, what's the diff."

Joey shakes his head at me. "Murphy, ya can't take that attitude. Some a those guys's probly dyin' in a state a mortal sin."

"Might be at that."

We lay low for a couple of days after that, figuring we're pretty unpopular with certain parties who are pretty well armed. Course, who knows how many are left alive.

So it's a welcome distraction when Sammy drops by, the guy that runs the gerbil races. Bunch a gerbils under a shoebox, middle of a circle, hoist the box and first one to cross the chalk line wins.

"Joseph! Michael!" Sammy is always in a good mood. "It is one week and I am not seeing you. The boys at the races have been pulling long faces: Where, they inquire, are the Brothers Murphy? You are perhaps otherwise occupied, writing your memoirs, compiling a written record of your many famous cases?"

"No, well, matter a that, there's some guys would like to write our memoirs *for* us."

He passes around the pretzel sticks, what he use stead of cigarettes or gum. "So where have you two gentlemen been hiding yourselves?"

"*Hiding*?! Who said we were hiding??!!! We been on vacation!"

"Oh! Ah. The Murphys, on vacation. Now, that is new."

"Whaddaya whaddaya — hadda go give the dog some fresh air."

"A generous sentiment; complicated by the fact that you gentlemen do not actually possess a dog."

"Okay so — we went camping! Mother Nature and stuff."

"Oh! All very new." Then he changes the subject, which is jake with us; and he tells a long and involved, purportedly funny story about a dog and a rabbi; and we attempt to laugh, but we sound like the tolling of a death-knell in the fog. Sammy clucks his tongue and breezes off.

I look at Joey.
"Is it that bad?"
"Yes it's that bad."
Cause what we do, when it gets That Bad — when booze won't do it, and dames can't hack it, and we can't hardly even take an interest in a barroom brawl —
when we've almost lost hope, at the end of our rope—
is ... we go feed the ducks.

There's this pond, west of the city, nobody hardly goes. Not marked and not right off a road. Just some rubble, then like a meadow, with like tires in it, and mattresses, and then some trees: and you go in there, and you go past it, and there's this pond.

Nothing on it. Bits of litter around the edge. Then dense trees beyond it, and vines, no path to it or through it, the wilds.

And if you stand there, with an offering — by and by these six white ducks float slowly out of the forest. They are solemn, and they make no sound. They just glide, smooth and slow, slowly right over to you, smoothly moving over the pond. And they accept your bread, one piece each; and then they turn around, and slowly glide home.

We drive in the general direction; park; and walk the last quarter of a mile.

We stand at the pond, our bread in our hand; and we feed them, three each. And we stay there for a long time after they are gone.

We walked back towards the car, silent for a while.

"You know, Joey — Sometimes I fantasize, that He will come back; and he'll walk through this stinking city, and see what a mess we made of it. Only it won't look the same to Him as it does to us — all the billboards with faded pictures of people smiling on them, so happy about their cigarettes; and all the neon lights — He'll see past all the glitter, and see things as they really are. And then one day, He'll be walking along and He'll notice this stagnant pool of barf in the gutter. And He'll think: oh my, a pool of barf. But then He'll look closer, and He'll see: No; no; sakes alive: it is Murphy's soul. And He will pick my head up into His lap, and He will stroke my hair: and He will be sad over me. And I'll look up, and I'll believe.

"You already believe, Murphy. You just don't know that you believe."

We walked the rest of the way in silence.

***

The next day we started looking again looking for Mallow. He was still just a loose thread, but we'd given it a tug or two, and all this stuffing had come out. It had turned out to be an interesting thread to pick at.

I figured the travel agency would be good for another visit. First time I went I hadn't known jack-spit; but now I had a hole-card. If Willie was even indirectly connected to Mallow, he was at least an outlier of a satellite of a hanger-on of this smack shipment. And the shipment was somehow a very big deal, bigger even than the raw tonnage of it. Wheels within wheels. Something that heavy would send ripples quite a distance when it crashed and splashed; and some of it would wet Willie.

One thing that I did not know was whether the deal as it now stood, with one-off windfall profits and a surrounding circle of violent deaths, was a carrot to him, or a stick. I figured I'd shake it at him and see if he salivated or if he couldn't find his spit.

Mallow might have been in touch with him. If he'd heard of his wife getting iced, he'd want the scoop, and Willie was a contact in the area.

I drove over slow, thinking how I'd do it this time. Maybe best not say anything, just give him this private smile, just keep drilling him with the cold knowing eyes, nodding A-*ha*! (like Pooh with the heffalumps), till he breaks down and starts to babble. But when I got there, the agency was boarded up. From what I could tell from behind the boards, it looked bombed-out.

Bombed and abandoned. I went to a phone booth and rang its number: disconnected, no new phone.

Well now this was a bit of a setback. But you just gotta keep on keepin' on — dealer deals the cards out, and you just play the hand. So I figured I'd drop by his home and chew the fat, just us girls, a little chat. Chances are he'd invite me up for a brandy and we'd chuckle over old times. Only, first thing was where did he live. Not in the phone book. Information didn't just say Unlisted, they said No such listing — probably have to pay extra for that.

But he hadn't necessarily always been unlisted. It's a hassle in some ways, to set that up; and he was probably in the book before he started feeling so much heat. I dug up some back issues of directories, and in one from three years ago, there he was: William Harfrock. Already at a very nice address, one you wouldn't soon move from just because you'd come into some extra dough. So I figured I'd blow by the place and see if he was still around.

I hopped in the 'iac and tooled over there, grooving on the neighborhood. I'd forgotten this town even had pockets like this. Acres of lawns, sprinklers twirling like ballerinas. Trees twice as old as I am. Houses set way back from the street, like distant memories.

Finally I come to Willie's place — and right away you see that something is wrong. A lawn as broad as the best of them but it hasn't been mowed. Chain-link fence around it with concertina wire on top — gotta be against the zoning, so he must have put it up just recently and the city hasn't had time to make him take it down. Shades drawn on every window. And in the front yard, snarling and unfed, a couple of pit bulls, looking like the hounds of hell.

I rummage in the trunk and get out some wire-cutters and a shotgun. First thing, I turn the dogs into hamburger, as a public service. Then I cut a little hospitality hole in the fence, and walk up the flagstone path to the front door. The flagstones do this cutesy little 'S' number on the way. I don't.

I lean on the doorbell but no answer. I give the door a gentle kick and the frame splinters. Deserted entryway. No butler scuttles up to take my visiting-card, so I shoot out the full-length mirror to announce my arrival. "Front and center, Willie."

Half a minute passes and I hear a shuffling. A screen of beads fills the doorway to the next room and a shadow fills it. I pull back behind a corner and level the Mauser. "No funny stuff, Willie. Hands where I can see them." He stumbles through.

He's wearing striped pajamas, and his dead-white hands are hanging limply at his side. His eyes are glazed and hollow. He hasn't shaved in days. He's thinner, which on him would look better, only the flesh that remains looks like drained paste.

He keeps coming towards me as though sightless, with stumpy steps. I gesture with the Mauser and want to shout for him to stop, but my saliva has dried and the voice won't cooperate. He just keeps coming — slowly, wavering, not a threat exactly, yet a thing of horror. Then he sinks to the floor, and embraces my knees.

"Please, please, I've told you everything." His voice too parched to be even a sob. "There is nothing left ... nothing left within me. Please please believe me ... or just kill, yes, yes kill me, please, just kill me ...." And then my stomach turns: for he is bending down, nuzzling the trousers, kissing the cuffs.

He does not know me. He doesn't recognize a thing. He has been worked over, over and over, by the experts, till he doesn't know which end is up.

Well, heck, that sucks, but still — no sense looking cross-eyed at a gift horse, as my pappy might've said. So I coolly light up a Camel, eyes narrowed against the rise of smoke, then slowly shake out the match. "You talked to my errand-boy. Now talk to *me*."

This does not have quite the desired affect: instead of pouring forth the Secret Plans, he breaks down blubbering. Not crying — not weeping — blubbering, something soft and moist and rubbery, quivering and heaving like rejected Jell-O.

I feel embarrassed for the guy, so I put out the cigarette, which has served its purpose, and fish around in my pockets to find him a piece of candy or something to distract him, and manage to come up with this cough drop, minus its wrapper, brush off

202

some of the little pocket particles and it's almost good like new. "Here."

He's so amazed, so grateful, that he stops crying. His eyes open, then he shuts them; then, still kneeling, hands still clasped, he puts out his tongue. — Eeyeuch, I'm really embarrassed now. "Pull yourself together," I growl.

I make him struggle up and hobble into the living-room. It's a cinch there'll be nothing left to find in this place — been gone over top to bottom by the pros. So I just start right in.

"Where was Richie Mallow's ticket to?"

"Paris, on Pan Am."

"Hotel at the other end?"

"No hotel."

Interesting. Either he was being met, or he was immediately traveling further, maybe to Marseilles.

Then inspiration.

"Where'd he get the drugs?"

Now Willie's voice became hysterical. "How should I know?" He cringed like a kitten, as if I was going to hit him. (Hey, keep this up and I just might.) "I mean, how *could* I know? It was you guys told me about it."

Hm. Okay. "Mallow have any relatives?"

"Just the wife that got iced."

Dang. I need *leads*.

I stood there awhile surveying this pitiful wreck of humanity — one that actually wasn't much to write home about even in its salad days — wondering what else he could tell me. Some aspect of the case I hadn't thought of? But then I'd have to know what to ask. Heck, he must be good for something. Maybe he knows some Polar Bear Jokes. — Meanwhile Willie waited patiently, meek as a lamb what's been pistol-whipped, sniffling from time to time.

"Who else is been in asking after Mallow?"

"Like I said before, there was the two guys came in even before Richie's wife got croaked, snooping around. The big dumb guy and then the little dumb guy that thought he was smart." I winced. Good thing I'd given him a phony card.

"Check. We already took care of them. Who else."

"Then a few days after the icing, Pasto come in — Nico's right-hand man."

I winced again. Nico would be needing one, seeing as how his own right hand I took off him.

"And what'd Pasto say?"

"Same as you, just Where's Mallow, and had I seen the two dumb guys specially the little one. I told him everything I could about those clumsy bums, playing at detectives with their little two-way wrist radios —"

Again I chafed. He still didn't recognize me.

"— and their stupid third-grade-dropout way of talking, and the enraging way that they still think they're so smart; and how if you wanted to find them and do the world a favor and rub them out, easy as pie

— just follow the stench of the Camels smoked like cheapskates right down to the lips —"

"Awright *awright*! Enough with the pen-portraits already. What happened then."

"And then ... this." He slowly pulled apart his shirt, gritting his teeth as more flesh tore away where it had melted together with the fabric, and I got to see a clinical demonstration of what a third-degree burn looks like after it has healed just part-way. Pasto had come at him with a flame-thrower. And it wasn't even Willie he was angry at.

I figured he'd been through enough and I was through with him, but before I left I figured I'd leave behind another red herring or two just to make things interesting, my signature calling card. Nico and Pasto were in town and they were looking for me.

"All right thanks, 'preciate it. Listen: We found out it was Nico and Pasto who set up the heist of Mallow's drug shipment. Only now they've had a falling-out only Nico doesn't know it yet and Pasto is just waiting till Nico's back is turned to plug him and muscle in on the whole scam. A lot of guys are gunning for them now, and they're out gunning for a lot of guys. You see either one of 'em, shoot 'em. Then call one of us."

I wanted to make things up to him a little but I was all out of cough drops. Well, tough luck, to one unlucky guy. I walked out the door and retraced my beeline back over the flagstones, whistling a tuneless tune.

***

When I told Joey, he didn't like it.

"I don't like it, Murphy. It's too complicated. We're getting too involved."

"No no no, you don't get it — I'm trying to get us *un*involved — get our Exit Papers. 'Cept of course for finding Mallow, we still gotta do that. Gumshoe's honor."

"How do you figure?"

"See, it's just a matter of time before some of the guys that want our scalps find out who it was that done 'em, and come hunting for us, make us into Murphyburgers. So we gotta keep their guns aimed at each other. So like see, I tell him the hit man and the hit boy pulled off the heist together. Next time the Mob chats with Willie, or maybe the other mob, he spills this; and maybe they think it's gen, and they go after Nico. Or at least question him and he naturally takes offense and ... Keeps 'em occupied."

"Yeh but, they got a photo or anything, or anybody know him, the guys at the docks can tell it wasn't them, cause it was us."

"Well, the docks guys done got shot up a bit. Plus it all happened so fast. And anyhow, that's just the one heist. I didn't say *which* heist. Let them guess about that. Cause it looks like there was another, over in Europe, that came up with that shipment in the first place. And it looks as though Mallow might have been involved in that scam, 'cause they sure as heck didn't get the stuff through the proper improper channels. Him or his buddies might of heisted it off of somebody else. So maybe they'll try to pin that one on 'im."

Joey keeps shaking his head, while my fantasies go orbiting around the air. "Murphy Murphy Murphy, these guys are mean. This ain't a game. And they can only be so dumb. And we can only be so lucky till our number comes up. Maybe we better take another powder, split town."

I stick my chin out. "Nobody runs *me* outa Dodge. — Look, Joey, I'll think a something."

So I go out and I drive around, looping around town; and pretty soon I get this loopy idea. I give it some gas and zap over to Sammy's.

He's at his usual haunt, pool room under his apartment. He's got a clutch of gerbils up on the pool table, trapped in the triangle, and the bets are down. First critter to the cushion wins; falls into a pocket, pays double.

I hang around and watch the action, then when the party breaks up, I motion him over.

"Why, Michael Murphy what an especial pleasure. Can I buy you a drink as I am newly rich."

"Thanks, Sammy, some other time."

"But by then I may be poor."

"I'll have to chance it. Listen, Sammy, you do me a favor?" I pulled him further into a corner, away from idle ears.

"Always I am wanting to do my friend a favor; some days two. And now you say I am to realize my dream."

"Good, just keep up that attitude. Lissen — there's this guy that I want to know how to get a hold of him, but it can't be me asking around or he might get a hold of me first."

"I perfectly understand. — I sense danger."

"You got that right — hey, you hang with me, you'll get to know its smell. But serious now: this guy's a bummer. You don't have to do this."

"And disappoint a good friend? Michael, I am hurt that you could think I would even think of it."

"Good on ya, Sammy. Now, you just ask around discreet and send out feelers; and when you get a lead, pull your feelers back in, or he'll chop 'em off for ya."

I describe Nico and mention Pasto though I couldn't really describe him, then I tell him we'll be in touch.

***

I told Joey, and he extra special didn't like it.

"Oh, Murphy, now you done it for real. Sammy's our best friend. You bring him into this?"

"Who, me? No see, he said — he told me —"

Joey just looked at me, with his seeing, sad eyes.

I hung my head. He was right. I'm a rat. Sammy what never harmed a flea, he just fleeced 'em. Hit-men like Nico were way out of his league.

"I'll call him back and tell him to forget it."

I tried, but no go. Already he was out.

"Maybe he's at El Toasto's, for the midnight brunch."

That's not far from here, so we headed out on foot.

The place was hopping, all right, but no Sammy, and no-one had seen him around. He was probably already out working on the case, on the favor that could dump him into the grave. O Murphy, O Murphy: what you done.

We roamed the nabe, checking out all the places he where he liked to hang: The All-Nite Laundromat that was closed during the day, with the extra-big dryers he likes to sit and watch sometimes, and sometimes to curl up in; the Magic Hamburger, where they cook them in these thin-thin disks and then stack them up like flapjacks; Joe's Poetry Barn, where anyone could get up on the crate and say his piece. But he was nowhere, nowhere.

We walked back the sad sidewalks, the still-winking neon of one of the closed places sending a green stain out on the pavement, shining in the light rain. Up ahead, on our side of the street, was St. Mary's, shut for the night. I started crossing to the other side of the street.

Joey hurried up behind me. "Hey, what gives?"

I shook my head. "I'm in a state of barf, you know that. Don't wanna get any of it on the church."

We walked on not saying anything, feeling so bad.

We get back to the flat the phone is ringing, it's three in the a.m. I fly to the phone, and it's Sammy, and he's alive.

"Is this the residence of Mr. Michael Murphy, and indeed of Mr. Joseph Murphy, equally?" he inquires in his invariable chirpy-imperturbable voice. From the way he talks, you can never tell, is he getting a b.j. or is he tied to the tracks.

"Sammy! thank God you're safe. Listen — case is called off, okay? All just a big misunderstanding, laugh about it later. Okay? You Okay? Where are you right now? We'll come get you."

"At the present instant I am situated at the bottom of a manhole, tapping into a phone line; a circumstance difficult to explain. I will not elaborate at the present time, as I intend to dine out on this adventure for several days; moreover there are certain gentlemen approaching —"

"Sammy!"

"— who might wish me harm. But set your mind at ease; my exit strategy is already in place; and though I say it as shouldn't, it is splendid. I will say only —"

"Sammy, forget it, *run!*"

"— I will say (as I was saying) only this: that the following digits may be of interest to you, unremarkable though each is individually. There are seven in all —"

210

"Sammy, *Sam*-myyy ...." Now I'm fighting back tears.

"— seven in all; and they have been chosen, each one, from among the ordinary roster of numbers from zero to nine."

"Sammy, for Christ's *sake* ...!"

But he went on unruffled as always, to recite the seven numbers, which drilled themselves into my brain like a death sentence.

"Take care," he concluded, "to preserve them strictly in the order given; since, permuted, though losing none of their individual charm, they would collectively yield much less interesting results. — And now I must go."

The phone at his end dropped with a clatter, and the sounds of sharp echoes like gunshots off rocks could be heard in the background; then the line went dead.

For a few moments, we are both of us too shocked to say anything. Then: "Oh-h-h Joey, oh-h-h Joey ... What I done. What I done."

He screwed up his eyes — not sympathizing, not cutting me any slack. "What he say?"

"Just a phone number. Plus, he's on the run."

Then a surprisingly practical suggestion, given that he had me on the hot-seat and could have kept me there. "We better call it, right away."

"It's ill-gotten gains."

211

"Like most of what most of us has got. We have to call it, we're in it this far; got to see what Sammy has got himself into."

I nod; I dial. It rings; I listen. Neither of us breathe. The ringing stops, there is a little whoosh of vacuum at the other end, like time escaping through a vent, but no-one speaks. There exists a waiting, with a certain indeterminate duration. Finally, casting hope into the darkness like a dart, I say: "Nico?"

There is a faint gasp, like air seeping out from burnt rubber, that seems to come from far away. Then he speaks, with a voice like red dust.

"I' … I' this th' guy … the wiseguy, the private eye…."

My heart is in my throat; then I collect myself, and try to rise to the occasion. "He-*hey*-ey, there, old buddy, you reconnize my voice?"

His I don't recognize; it is dry, dry. "I reconnize it anywhere," he whispers, like someone whose voice-box has been crushed. "I reconnize it in an alleyway; I reconnize it on a moonless night. I reconnize it, you on the moon, and me at the bottom of the sea. I reconnize it, me not yet born, just listenin' from m'mother's womb. You try t'disguise it — I reconnize it. You take a vow of silence — I reconnize your silence. I know you. I know how you taste; I know how you smell. I know what you dream about at night — *me*. And when I find you —"

"Say! Nicky, old sport — how's that hand?"

To my surprise, he gives a straightforward answer. "Well it's gone now, and there's still no feeling in the stump. But I been training up the other one, and now I'm almost as good a shot with the left. Plus that left — it always was my knife-hand, as you will shortly feel. And by 'shortly', I mean soon: but it will lassssst ... for a very long time."

"Hey, great! Y'know, I was thinkin' we might oughta get together. You know, thresh over old times. I was gettin' lonesome, thought you might wanna drop by and suck my dick."

Again the gasp; and then, almost as though savoring it. "O-oh-h ... yessssss ... Just keep talkin', just keep talkin' like that. It's jussst like I like it. I just wanna hurt you so bad, hurt you so bad that it *hurts*. Just keep on talking, music to my ears, great *Satan* I love to hear your voice! To hear it now, as it briefly is; and to savor it later, as it was, and never again shall be. When you can no longer speak; when you can no longer weep; when you attempt to retch, and even that is beyond you. When little dry salt-balls roll out of your tear-ducts as you ... beg me ... but you know you cannot beg me ... as you ... *pray* to me, yes, pray to me — cursing your mother and cursing your worthless punk of a god who cannot help you, cannot save you, will not lift one enormous little finger to save you from this world of pain. Cursing them and meaning it, hating your mother, cursing the mother of your worthless scarecrow of a god: while I slowly, deftly, twist the

213

knife, showing that my blade is stronger than your faith. Just keep pourin' in on, gasoline on the fire, *pour it on* —" His voice is still a singe'd whisper, but it's getting tenser, hotter, harsher and more hysterical.

"Hey, cool it, bud, this ain't dial-a-porn. You sound like you're givin' yourself a hand-job, there. — And I know which hand you're using, too, since y'ain't got but the one. Though I gotta hand it to ya, handsome, if you're as handy with your handle as you are with a handgun —"

He's screaming now, his vocal cords like rawhide on fire.

"Just - *name* it!! A place, a time! Name it, dammit — name it!"

Suddenly I'm all business; all the sass gone out. "Tuesday. Noon. In Center Square."

I hang up, suddenly exhausted, my t-shirt drenched in sweat.

"You're gonna *meet* him??" says Joey, incredulous. And then adds simply, "You a dead man."

"Well not exactly. Not in person. But we can't disappoint him. I reckon I'll send my entourage. Let's get together some people that he might like to meet. You cook us a burger while I work on the guest list."

He lumbers over to the hotplate, and pretty soon the skillet's sizzling with a couple of slabs.

I'm chewing my pencil. How to sculpt this social occasion? I shoulda paid more attention back in

Etiquette Class. Lessee ... There's the Scabrosos, of course: HQ in Florida but they got a local branch, just like a Howard Johnson's. They are probably the guys been messing with Willie. But how do I call them up? Yellow Pages under Mob? They got an 800 number? But then I remember this article from a few days ago, talking about the gang war, with all like names and things. I look around and finally find it, in the refrigerator, catching the drippings. I wipe it off. Yeh, here it is, Tony 'Big Tony' Scabroso, lives right here in town. I look him up and he-hey, there he is, right in the phone book, I mean what's he got to hide, a guy like that. Everybody knows what he does. The cops are in his pocket and he's happy for the listing, lets guys call him up what owes him favors.

So I call him. By now it's four in the morning. The man answers, sounding pissed.

"Say-Heyy, Fat Tony!" I check back at the news clipping. "I mean, Big. So how ya doin', Fatso — I mean, Big Guy?"

"Who the hell is this?"

"Oh hey, no way, no way to treat a buddy. It's *me*, Tony, it's me!" With any luck, I'll sound a little bit like some *one* of his pals, especially with the late hour and the bad connection.

"Who is this — is that you, Garfo?" he snarls. "You sound drunk."

"Oh hey, Tony, just beers is all, a man can't get drunk on just beers. Plus okay, some pills to keep me going. And some kind of ... powdery ... stuff ... I think ... But hey, Tony, I got you some news."

"Go on, spill it."

"O Tony, you'll love this. You know Nico? The guy that moved in on the heist?"

"Hey, hey, where'd you hear that?! I only just heard about that angle myself just a few hours ago!"

"No time, Tone, no time. But here's the scoop, the hot scoop of poop. Nico himself and his friends and relations are going to be at Center Square on Tuesday. And he's got his hands on your sister and he's going to bugger her right there in front of the cameras, at high noon."

"Why that — ! Okay, thanks, Garfo. We'll be there. Now lemme get some sleep. And get some yourself, you sound like shit. And lay off the damn powder, I already warned you about that. Catch you some beauty sleep and be there an hour early — bring your guys and bring your gats."

No no, no sleep for the just, or something like that. Gotta bring in the Morsue boys, *they* like to party hard.

And this one's a little harder. Their mob is bigger, but it's based across the waves, and half the guys they had in this town are by now probably stuffing up daisies. But whoever is left, there might be one or to back at the hideout, the one at the end of the alley behind the wooden door. So I go out to a phone booth and call a cabbie, pay him fifty up front plus one of the torn hundreds Louie gave me, other half when he gets back. I give him the message: The guys that swindled you are gonna be in Center Square on Tuesday, noon. He speeds off, supposed to meet me back here on this corner. Pity I don't got the other half of his hundred. Still, fifty's not bad for the trip. If he lives.

Shoot, there I go again, mixing an innocent person in with this. Well, not quite *innocent*, exactly, that particular cabbie. But Not Guilty on a technicality.

I head back to the office where Joey is snoring, cuddling a quart-sized beer-bottle under his arm like a teddy bear. I strip down to my shorts but cannot sleep. I just go over to the window, and lean on the ledge on my elbows, staring out over the sleeping city. A quiet night. Citizens, thousands of them, alone with their conscience in the black pit of slumber; dreaming, groaning, rolling over in bed.

And somewhere in a back room, a child will stir, — in pain, but not awaking. And its mother will hurry to its stifled cries, hastening to its side. The child cries out, its little fists aloft: The child is afraid of the lion. That beast, of whose fierceness he first learned in a story; but yet some buried instinct tells him, that they were somehow concealing something — that the beast is far fiercer than the story let on: and he is right.

The mother lays her hand upon the child's hot forehead; and soothes it, with sweet soft meaningless murmurs. And as the child, with one last whimper, sinks back into the shadowed comfort of a fitful sleep, she too looks out, across the streetscape, at the urban jungle, its alleys dark in the sink pit before the morning, its sidewalks raked by pale streetlights, its ranks and banks of unlit windows like blind eyes. The pitiless windows; the pitiful silent cries. So many were born; so many have died. Her lips, in silence, form the prayer: *Lion, lion, — spare my child.*

Chapter Eleven

Tuesday can't come too soon to suit me. I'm fired-up, but I'm nervous; snapping at Joey, messing things up. And still no word from Sammy.

I'm pacing up and down for the zillion-teenth time, when the phone rings. I dive for it. "Hellohello? Hello?"

No answer, and no hang-up. Just this vile little space of a wait. Letting me turn slowly on the spit here, roasting slowly over the low fire And then a chuckle. And not the kind where you're sharing a joke.

"Who *is* this?"

Another chuckle. "A friend of a friend."

"Yeh rilly? I doubt it. Friends of yours? No friends of mine. So like — spill. What's the deal."

"Deal? *Deal*? Yeh hey I like that. Took the words right outen m'mouth. So like, let's make a deal here. My side? I got like your friend here, and I figure — hey, maybe it's just me — that you just might want to have him back."

"Oh yeh rilly?? And which exactly friend is that?"

"Answers to the name of 'Broadway'."

... My blood freezes in my veins. 'Broadway': my sometimes nickname for Sammy, count of the way he talks; but just between him 'n' me. Everyone else, they call him 'Sammy', don't nobody else know about that name. So he's telling me something. First, the guy's really got him. Second, the guy doesn't know who he really is. Which means the guy doesn't know what he

219

does, or where he hangs out, and doesn't know me. But he clawed on to Sammy, which means it was probably tied in somehow with this Nico thing.

My throat is dry. I try to sound normal. "You got other friends too? Like, begins-with-an-N and rhymes-with-Rico?"

"What, that shit? He doesn't have friends, he just has victims. You almost oughta thank me, bringing your friend in like this. He was hanging around the cesspools where Nico likes to swim. 'Tain't healthy. Fact is, you will thank me, kindly, in cash."

Now, cash and Murphy are like oil and piss, you just can't mix 'em. Try like you might, they never stay together long. So Sammy must've told him something different.

"How much'll it be?"

"Weh-he-ell, you've got a head for business there, that you do. And you'll need it. The way I feature it, you got something to hide. Nobody goes around trying to hire Nico without they got, A, a guilty secret for what they gotta get someone rubbed out, and, B, another guilty secret that they hired the rubbing. Plus C, plenty of cash in nice anonymous small bills, because a trigger like Nico doesn't come cheap.

"Now, I don't know if this funny-talking runt means shit to you, but he knows what he knows, and if you don't buy him back, I might just let him blab. And until you fork over, he's not leaving and he's not dying; once you buy him, he's yours to do with like you like. I give you forty-eight hours to raise the jack. After that, you're not here, he starts singing, loud and clear. You read me?"

The wheels are spinning in my crazy head. "Yeh — yeh I read you. Name your price." What an irony — the guy thinks Sammy was my go-between to go *hire* Nico, for some filthy job, and that I'm willing to pay so I can get my hands on him and shut his trap. Well, let him think that. Right now, my position doesn't look too good; but any little thing that I'm clear on and he's confused, is to my advantage.

So: He thinks I'm loaded. Loaded with debts is more like it, but still, in the short term, his misconception is a plus. Buys me time. He thinks I want to hush things up and that I'm ready and willing to do business. That keeps Sammy alive and well.

And as a matter of fact, come to think of it — I *am* loaded. With dope.

"Skip the forty-eight hours stuff," I say in my best breezy businessman's voice. "How's a million sound? I can pay you tonight."

A gasp, then silence. Then: "A ... *million*. Why, that's what I call handsome! You must really like your little friend. Yes, an even million; that would be most satisfactory, sir. Most satisfactory indeed." He can't believe it could be this easy; and then, indeed, suddenly, he doesn't. "You don't mean pesos, right? That's in US dollars?"

"Actually, I mostly do my banking in bullion and Swiss francs. But the way my funds are tied up right now, from Switzerland to the Caymans, it'd take me a week to get my cash back from the laundry. But I can pay you in something that's better than money. I can pay you in smack."

At once he realizes he's out of his league. But he doesn't dare fold — he can't crumble. "In … *smack*."

"Yes, the big H, as pure and as white as the driven snow. Not shittin' ya. Run a chemical test right in front of you if you like, bring your own trusted chemist. And if it's not the best you ever seen — so good you won't even want to sell it, you'll want to keep it for special occasions, leave some for your grandchildren — if it's not the tangiest, tastiest smack in town, then you can have 'Broadway' for lunch."

"All right. Tonight. Now my … my regular chemist in these matters, he's out of town just at present, had to see a fellow about a dog. But I trust you. Eight o'clock, say?"

"Eight. On the dot. Meet you front of police headquarters."

"Front of *what*?"

"What — you got a problem with that? The one place no-one tries any funny business. Plus half the guys are on my pad — they'll probably bring us hot coffee. So — be there or be square. And bring the package."

"Okay, okay …." Shaken.

222

I hang up. Not a bad bit there, Murphy. Pretty smooth; y'oughta be on teevee. First the guy thinks you're some scumbag in a jam; then he thinks you're a big business wheel, calls you 'sir'; and now he knows you're sitting on millions in smack, just lying around the playroom it would seem. So you must be rough stuff. Likely you got a mob behind you; or if you don't, then you're a crazy man, and twice as dangerous. Up to him, he was probably going to demand ten gees and you could jaw him down to five. Then you called and raised and trumped him with a million, out of nowhere. Blew him out of the water — clean wiped his mind. The way you got him rattled now, he'd probably settle for two bits in trading stamps, IOU's gladly accepted, credit not a problem, "I will gladly pay you Tuesday, for the hostage today", he'll just be glad to escape with his skin. Yeh, this is fun.

I grab a grocery bag and walk out to the truck, whistling. Lump lump lump, Will that be all, ma'am? Then I stuff some in the glove compartment of the Pontiac, and some under the seats, and I go get Joey. Won't he be happy to hear what I've done. Looks like we're gonna squeak by on this one. Sammy come home.

When I tell Joey, he doesn't say anything. Probably thinking of Sammy in danger, and Murphy's soul in danger. Of the sin and the sickness and the silliness of it all. Don't know what is in his head. But I notice he's got his rosary going.

As for me, I'm acey-deucey. We even go out for supper, have some nice lasagna in a little place not too far from police headquarters. We have our last glass of Chianti a little after eight; and then — fashionably late — indulge in a little post-prandial stroll and then settle comfortably in to the 'iac. We drive slowly over to headquarters and circle the block a few times. Not much happening — streets pretty much deserted at this hour in this part of town. Then before long we notice that another van has been doing the same thing — both vehicles slowly circling, one clockwise one not, passing in the night. We park by the hydrant and I get out. The other van double-parks beside us. I mean, you can't get much more innocent than that.

I'm dressed for the part — after all, it's a show — creased pleats, dark shirt, white tie, and a carnation in the buttonhole, so purple it's almost black. A huge ring on the middle finger — the gold happens to be fake, but a trinket that gaudy would look fake in any case.

This ratty guy comes over, eyes going this way and that, licking and licking his lips. There is no-one around to overhear us, but he speaks in a low tone. "You got the stuff?"

"Who's asking, asshole?" Pressing my luck to the floor.

He startles, he's not used to this: but he sees me leaning, sneering, dressed kinda dago, arms folded, hands where he can see them, not having bothered to bring backup, just not a worry in the world.

"A friend a your buddy," he says, biting his lip and looking at the ground.

"So fork over the buddy."

"And ... the white stuff?"

My eyes get narrow, hard little slits. "I say fork, I mean fork."

He shudders, goes back and unlocks the van. Sammy steps out, as though from a bandbox, a tad crumpled, but smiling and dusting off his sleeves, looking pleased. He spots my get-up, and cottons-on immediately.

"Godfather! When is this that you get in from your voyage to the island nation of Sicily?" He embraces me, delicately kisses both cheeks. "I hear, to my chagrin, that you have been having some trouble there."

"Yeh, my old boyhood buddy the undertaker, his business been falling off. So I drop by, find out there's some guys they got wise, and now he's got more business than he can handle. — Say who is this stiff?" I jerk a thumb at his hapless kidnapper.

"Ah! This gentleman is my very good friend; *his* very good friends call him 'Slinky'."

"Good friend a yours, huh? That's good, cause anybody not a good friend a my friends, I just might get unfriendly."

Slinky is smelling like he could use a john.

225

"So hey, friendly guy," I say, turning to him and smiling. "Here's the white stuff, just like I promised."

His eyes bug out. He cannot believe it. Not only am I letting him get out of here alive, but I'm doing this crazy giveaway.

"It's real. Here, taste it." I dip my finger in and swish it around, then shove it deep into his mouth.

He nods, his eyes like twin blue moons above some other planet. He sucks, and he keeps on sucking, until I let him off the hook and pull my finger out.

But I'm not done playing. I place the bag in a strongbox and lock it. I hand him the strongbox and show him the key, which I keep.

"I like you give a message to friend Nico. I'll know about it when you tell him; and when you have done it, I leave the key in that phone booth across the street. Box not much good to you without the key — it's wired to explode if you try to jimmy it. And the key's no good to me without the box, plus I don't care about the box, what I want is you do what I want. Capisc'?"

He nods quickly several times, then his mouth forms the meaning, What message.

I look at him long and slow. "You go tell Nico, and you say it nice and slow with letter-perfect elocution so he'll understand, Okay? You tell him ... that his *mother* ... You got that? ... His ... *mother* ... ... s-s-**sucks** ... a ... dawg's ... asshole ... — You tell him that, word for word."

He's looking at me wildly, gazing with horror at the box. It could contain all the rubies of India, wouldn't be worth it to tell Nico that.

I sneer at him. "So tell him on the phone if you're yellow. But don't worry about him, he won't hurt you, he's just a punk. I done punked him, plenty of times, bent over a barrel. You just tell him that, with compliments of the Scabrosos. That's Sca-bro-sos. Tell him the Scabrosos told him that."

He gulps, nods, and scrambles back into the van. The stench of his fear mingles with the stink of burnt rubber as he peels out. In his haste, he forgot the heroin.

"Really and truly, Michael, you should be on Broadway," says Sammy as we stroll off, abandoning our borrowed vehicle, since it's a nice night. "Ah — Broadway! Where my heart remains down to this very day."

"Matter a fact, I can offer you front seats at a show that'll knock your eyes out. Or somebody's eyes out. You free for lunch on Tuesday?"

"Tuesday, Tuesday ... Allow me I consult my busy calendar." He does a brief comedy of rolling his eyes back into his head, as if to read something posted there. "Yes yes. I had planned to attend my mother's funeral at that hour; but for you, I can break a date. And Sammy still has all his green dollars, as Slinky returns them for some unknown reason after he calls you on the phone. So as I offer you the last time, I am buying."

"N-ho, Sammy, believe me: this one's on me."

Tuesday comes as it must, panting like a dog on the heels of Monday. We all three of us drive over a little early and get a table on the terrace of the Café Central. Ringside seats for today's entertainment.

Now, Center Square isn't central to just anyone; the Quality's got otherwhere to hang. It is only certain portions of the population that come here to Center to meet and greet, to see and be seen. Or, on today's playbill: to slay and be slain.

For regulars, you got your soused-out winos stumbling in from Skid Road. You got the leftover cokeheads and holy fools filtering in from Bleak Street. You got the sharp guys and the hustle boys, striding in from Graft Alley. You got the pimps and their prosties strolling in from Lust Lane. You got the geeks and the freaks and the dog-walkers flushing in from Wideway. And you got the pushers slinking in from Smack Avenue, trailing addicts like ducklings behind the mother duck.

And today, somehow the sunlight, the square is more festive, more crowded than usual. It is as though the word had somehow gotten out. Gamblers and their girlfriends, dressed to the nines, are settling in around the edges. A tour bus, normally destined for Atlantic City, today has come here instead. Gawkers and onlookers — shape-shifters, sharpers — everyone's come to the Fair.

I order three beers and put in an order for three more to come ten minutes later, and three more again ten minutes after that. Sort of like a time-release capsule.

"Well, Sammy," I say, sucking the foam off the first one. "Wanna tell us about your escapade?"

He hoists his glass and says, "Cheers to one and all," and delicately drains a little layer of it. Then he dabs his lips with his napkin, and adds:

"No doubt you are referring to my solo escape through the city sewers, my battle with the alligators, and my ultimate capture by the crazed bondage minions of Molnor, the garbage king. But the day is young and the sun is as you will notice still brightly shining; I must leave my dark tale for another and more dismal day."

"Yeh, I getcha, save it, wrap it up and keep it fresh. Wouldn't want it to get interrupted: 'cos in ten minutes, we are going to have us *some fun.*"

Joey looks at me quizzical. "How come you're so hepped up for this, Murphy? I mean, I want to see Nico arrested as much as you do, but it's like you're having fifty years worth of birthdays all at once."

"Say hanh? — I mean, it's going to be an arresting spectacle, but not like you mean. Probably no actual arrests."

"But — those calls you made. I thought you were inviting the cops!"

229

"Oh! Well, no, they couldn't make it. Thought you might like to get a gander at the Scabrosos, plus our old pals from the Morsue. Kind of like a family reunion. A dysfunctional family."

"Murphy, that's crazy! They'll kill each other! I thought you was just calling the cops!"

"Aww, Joey, what would be the point of that?"

Joey is speechless; but Sammy, unexpectedly, comes to my defense.

"Your brother is correct, Joseph," he observes, very polite and reasonable. "To bring together upon one single proscenium, Mr. Nico and the officers of the law, would in no wise produce high drama. They would give a little bow and say, 'Good day to you, sir, Mr. Nico, we hope and trust that you are well.' And he would say, 'Smatta wichoo, I get this parking ticket on my getaway car?' And they say 'Sorry sir just give us the name of the rookie patrolman who did this thing and we shall bust him down to pooper-scooper duty.' And he says 'Plus you gotta do something about this terrible traffic problem, all the time I get caught up in tie-ups as I am making my escapes.' And they say, 'We get right on it, Mr. Nico, and in the meantime we offer a police escort.'"

"Yeh, real funny," says Joey. "But you get all these guys in a single corral and there's gonna be a shoot-out, with blood in the dust."

"Hm, think that might happen?" I put in. "So okay, so we say a Mass for their departed souls." Joey scowls and I get serious. "You want the facts straight: Fact is, those guys, they been starting to get on my case. Always following us and shooting at us and threatening us and stuff — and you oughta see what they did to old Willie. And these Center Square types, hey, it'll make their day, they'll just scarf it all up with mustard."

"A tasty combination," approves Sammy, "and a timely reminder that we ourselves must procure some fresh popcorn to go with this." He signals for a waiter, who inclines his head and then goes next door and buys some from a sidewalk vendor.

"Murphy, Murphy, sometimes, you can be a rilly hard guy. — But *you*, Sammy — where do you fit in? So gentle with the gerbils, always square with a guy. Never raise your voice, never hurt a fly. So where do you get off, lapping this up like that? I mean, what is it with you two?"

Sammy gives a little frown, which is not at all like him; and then speaks in a serious tone.

"You see, Joseph, your brother is a fallen man, Mankind after the Pratfall. You, you are just; and you may make so bold as to judge him. But I myself — I am not of that world. A bad sort I am not (you must take my worthless word for this), but I lack all knowledge of good and evil. I simply have no truck with it, one way or the other. I live by my merry wits."

Joey's shaking his head — this is either too deep, or too shallow, by half. "Still but I mean, *Murphy*, I mean — setting all this up, and then just coming in and kicking back like you're at some ball-game, to take it all in ...."

It's been a rough couple of weeks, on top of some rough months prior to that; and I'm starting to get hot under the collar. "Hey lissen, y'know, I ain't got a m'nopoly on that. What about the Big Guy, huh, sittin' up there on his pile o' clouds, staring down on us bimbos, bumping into one another and bumping each other off; having a Fall, dropping the ball; sinning up a storm, driving off of cliffs? How does *He* get *His* jollies, huh?"

"That's blasphemy, Murphy."

"Maybe it isn't and maybe it is. But it works both ways. See, Sammy here opts out of the good-and-evil game entirely, he's just lucky that he's got decent instincts. You, *you* want to hunker down in the Good and just shut your eyes to the rest of it all — to nine-tenths of everything that's going on around us, and been going on and going down, ever since the Apple — and somehow that's hunky-dory."

"Hey that's not fair —"

"I don't care is it fair. You had your way, we'd all still be back in Eden. Clueless and naked and glad *of* it. But see, me, *me*, I got - to - know - *both*. Good and Evil, right down to the bone — sucking out the marrow, and licking it. It'd been me, I'd a eat the whole Apple and spit out the pits. And then maybe go hunt me up an Orange."

(Murphy staring hard, at the table, as he says this, staring at something unseen.)

"Good and Evil. I got to know both of them. Man it's, I don't know, it's like eatin' *pussy*, I just can't help it, I just wanna know how it *tastes*."

Joey steams and is silent. Then he says: "Well, watch out what you ask for, cause you're about to get a mouthful. There's Nico, and he's got guys with him, and they're looking mean and packing heat."

And sure enough, there's a black sedan at the side of the square, in a kind of sidewise variation on parallel parking: it has its rear wheels parked up on the sidewalk, a Gatling gun mounted on the hood. Nico's in the front passenger seat, staring straight forward. His face looks thinner, as from some gnawing inner sickness or wasting-disease; and there have been other changes. His right arm is fitted out with a prosthesis, lying lax along the door where the window's rolled down, and it ends in twin sharp black hooks.

"Some more buddies," points out Joey, as the next round arrives — arriving right on the dime with our second round of beers. Six sleek limousines. blindingly black and clean, draw up at the opposite side of the square. The doors all open, and the hard guys get out, taking up positions behind the armor-plated doors. The Scabrosos for sure.

Now that's a little unusual — for gangsters up in their class, this counts as slumming. And the regulars notice this and sort of start to filter on back to the sides and the sidewalks, and take up posts in doorways and scout out the scene. The tough guys smoke but otherwise don't move a muscle. And pretty soon the whole central part of the arena is silent and empty, with just a bit of litter blowing across.

And now at the far end, four more battered cars, all miscellaneous, not a disciplined gang, nose in. I recognize Hawkeye in a pick-up, his gun arm in a sling. But his left is cradling an Uzi.

And now some other guys I don't recognize. Maybe a scratch team of local muscle, maybe just unemployed toughs from the projects, up for some action, or who knows, some high-school hoods, heard about this somehow ona radio.

The sun shines down like spotlights, and the asphalt simmers and we feel the heat. Almost motionless, we slowly sip our beers. The waiters have noticed that something is up, and they stand at attention, looking out, their white napkins draped over their arms.

Time ticks like an insect.

A fly settles on the rim of an espresso demitasse; fusses about a bit; and then, somehow obscurely satisfied or refreshed, takes off the same way it came.

Wordlessly, glances are exchanged.

While all around the perimeter, new teams arrive and are setting up shop, checking their weapons, synchronizing their watches, arranging barricades.

And then, from stage right,
: there comes a woman walking, pushing a stroller,
: one step in front of the other,
: having no idea.
She seems to notice nothing, just calmly walking forward, mother and child, enjoying the sunshine — though the breeze has died.

A subdued ripple of excitement passes through the onlookers, like a low wave unfurling along the beach. This could be interesting, they think.

"What the **hell** is she doing in this part of town!" I start from my seat.
Around the sunlit edge of the square, no movement. In the darkness of doorways, people placing bets.

The woman keeps coming, the baby asleep in its little nest in front of her, rolling quietly into the square. She is dressed in pale green cotton, and white gloves. Her hat has a veil, which is pinned back. Low heels — sensible shoes. Noticing nothing.
Nico's gun hand now holds a gun — holding it in his hooks.

(Murphy now sees his life passing before his eyes; and he does not like what he sees.)

The Scabroso dons you can't figure what they're up to, behind their tinted glass; but their outside gunsels now seem more alert, and have tossed away their butts. The Morsue mob is getting itchy and they're pointing their gats this way and that.

And in the clear still air of highest noon, in the silence like a surrounding sky, you can hear, as clear as the cry of the lark, the sound of a hammer being cocked.

My heart goes cold as ice and as clear. I leap over the railing and sprint towards her, waving my arms and screaming, screaming, "*Get back! Get back! Get back!*"

Nico spots me and jumps out of his car. The way they tell it later, he had his marksman's pistol in his rebuilt right hand, and a big friendly Thompson in his left.

The woman just stares at me like I'm a madman, and she's not far wrong. Screaming and flailing and racing and wailing — She is stock-still, in horror: not at the unknown dangers that face her, but at this figure out of a blood-red dream. Instinctively she moves between me and the stroller, to shield it.

The Scabrosos don't know me for Bozo, they got no beef; but they have spotted Nico, and they wish he should cease to exist. A shot rings out.

The woman is too focused on the wildly approaching stranger even to notice this. She raises an arm as though shielding her face from the sun, which indeed is in her eyes now — but I lunge past her and scoop up the stroller.

All eyes are on us from the surrounding stands.

The Morsue mob, some of them know me some of them don't, but Hawkeye won't quick be forgetting my mug. And anyone who recognizes me, out there smack dab in the center of the sun-drenched square, will want a piece of me. But on the other hand, now they have noticed the Scabrosos, who in turn have noticed them; the rival gang that they've been tangling with small-scale in alleyways over the last couple of weeks. So it's kind of like the donkey between two bales of hay.

I'm running like hell on heels, holding up the stroller and shielding it best I can with my chest, while the mother runs after me, shouting for me to stop. I fly to the side of the square and barrel off down a side-street, the woman in close pursuit, and actually gaining on me since the stroller is heavy. Behind us, the bullets are flying everywhere now.

We get safely out of range, around a building, and I stop, sweating and heaving and panting. I turn, and hold out the stroller. She snatches it, thinking I'm a kidnapper who's just given up because he's out of shape. Still I just stand there, empty-handed. She looks down at her baby and then back at me. And all the fury of all the mothers who have ever seen their babies in danger; who ever have sensed the menace peering out at them from the darkness with glittering eyes; who have learned to fear the senseless sudden savagery of strange solitary males; — it is all just balled up within her, like a fist of fear, and she lashes out and strikes my cheek, her wedding ring opening up a gash. I just stand there, eyes pressed shut, the little hot tears oozing out around the corners. And then slowly, I turn the other cheek.

She raises her other hand and then it hangs there as she at once perceives the gunfire and the shouting and the grenade explosions back at the Square. And she is disoriented and I just stand there and her hand sinks and she looks down at her child, who, would you believe it, is still sweetly asleep, all that jouncing around as I carried the little fella just sends them deeper into dreamland; and she looks back at me and at last, she understands. *Ecce homo.* Then she perks up lightly on her tiptoes, shivering, and plants a kiss where the cheek is still bleeding, and hurries off.

Back at the square it's still all shouts and shooting and things blowing up; and then sirens and getaways, gravel spitting from spinning wheels, while the crowds are cheering, heaving caps into the air, and getting into the spirit of things with little scuffles of their own, laughing and crashing through storefronts and hurling little things they've looted, things looted only to be thrown. And eventually even the cops have to get involved, sighing and setting aside their final donuts, wading in with nightsticks flailing, flailing as though threshing the standing corn, listlessly into the throng. And then they go around with little notebooks, picking up lies from the bystanders; while the EMT's cart the bodies off.

"You want to stay for the credits?" asks Sammy when I rejoin them, but I shake my head.

"Let's just call it a day."

Sammy heads off his own way and me and Joey drive in silence, slowly home. I'm still sweaty and shaking from how close it came.

We get to the flat and Joey gets out and heads up still not saying, maybe he's not speaking to me, while I sit in the car, too tired to move, as though frozen in stone. Then he turns on the stairs and glances back at me and shakes his head, then heads on up and is gone. Me I'm just sitting in the beat-up old auto, drooping and tired of life.

I eventually hoist myself out and start walking across town, through the empty avenues, past the lately-blooming greenness of young trees. I have to strike out across the waste places — to hike, to hide, to heal the spirit. And I wander till I wind up where all roads lead, down at the abandoned tire-yard.

Everywhere else in town, the last rain's last waters have dried; but not here. This here is the land of the low-lying places; the places that have sumps, and dug-out spots, and gullies. It collects in the tire-hollows, dwells on the ledges; with traces, rain-worn into the dust, traces like the tracks of tears.

All the runoff from the surrounding rubble flows on down here, bringing with it the scent of the streets. It collects in brown pools, splotched at the bottom of clay slopes the color of sunburn. It's the city's bathwater, hoarding up the traces of what everyone else has shed and forgot. Man, I could just ... *wade* in it ....

I stand there, panting, walled away, fingers hooked in the diamonds of the wire link fence. Nobody's down there. No-one ever is. I sort of pump my arms, and the whole fence pulses, wa-*doom*, wa-*doom* ... the only thing that moves. The sun is silent but it never lets go, shooting down its photons, take *that*andthatandthatandthatand**that**. But it all just rolls like butter off the pile of tires.

No breeze, don't need no breeze here. No shadows, and no clouds. Everything is perfect, just exactly as it is.

This is yours, Murphy. You don't remember it, but you feel like it's the first thing you ever saw in this world; as it will be the last. Somebody just somewhy, set you down on this planet, smack here in front of these tires. And whatever else may happen, whatever roads you go ... : it always comes right back down to this. No-one's ever down there, nothing ever moves. And still the pile rises. No-one comes, and no-one goes,

but still it climbs, higher and higher. And you, you just keep
    striking out,
    into the wide world, and circling back here:
standing stranded, standing staring, through the chain-links, at the tires.

    And come one day, when your luck in this life has run low; when that candle gets to guttering, and you can feel the ticker flickering, — maybe bleeding five different places from a hard-guy's Ruger .22 —
    you're gonna crawl right up atop that tire-pile;
you're going to say you are so sorry, for every last thing;
you're going to offer up your spirit, as you might offer a bowl of soup to someone thirsting; —
    while the sun burns fury, blazing its heat rays from its hot red angry eye,
    until the tires ignite, and your heart takes flight,
    and you expire, upon a pyre of tires ....

Chapter Twelve

And so the weeks go by, and the town's pretty quiet, count of half the hard guys done gone bought the farm. I keep an eye out for word of Mallow, checking the news items, obits, even the personals. (Like: "Lost: Two tons heroin. Call Richie for reward." Or: "Gangster, widower, seeks compatible mate.")

I hunted up LaBelle's girlfriends, such as she had, asked them what they knew of Mallow; but just from that little, as much as I knew, it was all just made-up stuff, and self-deceiving lies.

I also asked a number of people flat out: Did you know Mallow? This meant a higher profile than I'd had before, just snooping around; but no matter, the heat was off; and caution, I cast that to the winds. Nico was dead; dead (so I'd heard) now was Hawkeye; Louie: dead; The Morsue remnant had got the worst of it, there in the Square, the survivors fled to France; the Scabrosos had suffered a little population control of their own, and those that lived to tell the tale were back in the swamplands of Florida, licking their wounds. Willie I'd heard committed suicide. Everyone else was lying low, or permanently out of the game.

It was surprising how few people really knew anything of substance about Mallow. A lot of people had heard of him, or met him briefly in this connection or that — sometimes under the name of Richard Malheureux or Ricardo Malo — but he hadn't sunk in, he was vague; and now that he was gone, he just kind of rolled out of their lives. That sort of depressed me.

The way the guy could just disappear, without a widow to mourn him, or ditched girlfriend to curse him — neither creditors, to seek him out; nor witnesses, to point him out, be it in a lineup, or in a morgue — well it started to get to me. It's as though the waters had just closed over his head. Everyone else was thrashing about, drowning, crying out for help, getting eaten by sharks: but from where he'd disappeared, not even a bubble.

I mean ... do we even leave footprints, as we walk these sands? If you prick us, we bleed: but does the blood turn to dust, to red dust, to blow away on the wind, at the first breeze? When we cry, do the echoes die? When we weep in our solitude, does anyone hear at all — or do even the angels turn away?

Joey had lost interest; but for me, it was grinding away inside. I started taking out personals in the big-city papers — first here, then all the way to the Coast; and then (in English) in the papers of the capitals of Europe; and at last, in all the languages known to Man, in leaflets and broadsheets, in flyers and supermarket giveaways — billboards, graffiti, banners trailing behind biplanes: asking, pleading, for anything, about Mallow: no detail too small. Selling off stuff or hocking it to pay for the ads: until our office was bare, stripped, right down to the door and the windows. The ads —

244

some were threatening, some were begging; some held out the hint of a great reward. And we did after all still have his smack in the back of the truck, his sole memento. I even spent evenings at my friend's who's a ham — beaming out messages into the ether: *Richie Mallow — Call Home — Call Home Richie — Call Home ....*

And while waiting for an answer — the answers never came — I used to go on walks, long walks, and think about the guy. A guy I never met and never knew, who yet has meant so much in my life. Long walks through woods — through wilderness; long walks, that lasted many nights and days. And all for nothing — all for dust and ash. Because I don't know the first thing about him — never met him — don't know what he *eats*; don't know what he *smokes*; don't know where he *hangs* ... Don't know the first thing. And as the days waned, and the stars grew bright — I might gaze up into the firmament, amid all the stars — the Great Bear; the Little Bear; and lo, Orion, mighty hunter of the winter skies. Do you — any of you — are you, *any* of you — — *Mallow*? Remember or resemble ... *Mallow*? Or has he become a constellation unto himself; died, and been placed among the stars ....

***

Then one day, trudging, I get back to the flat, and there's a letter for me, postmarked out of Indiana. It's from — shut my mouth — from Timmy. Timmy what I'd almost forgot.

Allow me to fetch my reading-spectacles (for many years have passed, since these events took place, fixed forever in the amber of time), and I shall read it aloud.

Dear Mister Murphy

Hi its me — timmy.

You probibly wonder how i know your name, anyway the name you use at this address. Must of bin when you was makin up that packij for me — thanks — that packij, what you — maybe you was drunk, but anyhow a buncha stuff fell in. Their was a stick a gum, a part of a comb, some pizza crust, an old rubber, I mean a *rilly* old rubber, what a yoo doo, you use em over again? And plus other stuff, but, the main thing, is : your P.I. card. Says M + J Murphy - Private Investigators - plus something I forget. And then it gives this address that I am writing to you at.

You probally wonder what happen after that. I hit the city like you said, only it turn out to be this little town. And I'm holed up, hiding out, and a week goes by, and nothing happens, and it's like, their's nothing to hide from. So I go outdoors and blink my eyes. Then stuff happens, maybe I tell you about it if we ever meet again. And then later I open the parcel, which I hadden done before because it wassen address to me, but I coulden give it to anyone else because of one thing,

246

there issen any State Street there. And then I find your note. That was a lot of money.

I got a job at a soda fountain just to think it all thru, and well, to short out the story, I met a girl, a rilly nice one, and now we're hitched. We got ourselves a little cottage, and mostly all a the money is left over, the simple things dont cost is much here. So then I relize, I dont even need it, so I give it all to the church, this program they got, to help out somother guys with a grubsteak. Cause there's a lot of guys got it a lot worse than I do, me I have everything I could ever want.

So I guess I got to thank you Mr Murphy. Even though you are one crazy guy. The way you were bopping around, like, rill dimentid, I was thinking you might oughta get some kind of a therape or a serape or something. But I guess you got some good in you cause you staked me when I needed it and I went and got a good job in a garage and Norma, that's my bride, she's expecting a little child.

So, well, so long, and God bless.
Timmy

I finish reading this, I get kind of lumpy, this is the best thing that has happened since, well, since I don't know when. But Joey, he didn't know Timmy like I knowed Timmy, so he thinks the whole thing is pretty funny.

"He-eyy, Murphy, looks like you done some good after all. Boy, God sure works in some str-r-r-a-a-aange ways. He'll even use *you!*" I swat him with a newspaper and he goes off chuckling.

And me I'm here still sitting here. Staring out the window with the dust on it in streaks. Staring through the busted screens. Staring past the haze of the streets, to where the sunlight bounces off the empty store-front windows opposite — brilliantly, blindingly, like a bomb.

A white fence ....

I can almost, sort of sense it, their kid going back and forth, back and forth on a swing. The little kid is laughing, but you can't hear it, it's like behind glass. And it's almost as though I remember it, from a long time ago: only I know that that never happened to me....

The kid — it's a little girl, I can see that now. With like ... blonde ... curls ... and a blue ribbon in them. And a white pinafore. And it's like, I want to talk to her, I want to say something but I can't. And she's still swinging and I'm standing, stammering, so near but somehow way in the background, she cannot see or hear me — me, standing three foot tall in stocking feet, standing four years old on Maple Street: sweetly needing, deeply bleeding: needing her, not knowing her, and needing to know.

My head goes down in my fists and now I'm back at this time at this table, this chair. This room with the sagging ceiling and the floors that are bare.

Me. Michael Murphy. This Is Your Life.

***

For a while after that, we put the case officially out of our minds, though it was always in the back of mine. For a while, underneath the surface, there had been this little patch of coolness between Joey and me, on account of the stuff I'd said — not so much the stuff about him, as about what he believed in. But we pretty much patched it up, see cause with us, each guy, the other guy is the main thing he's got.

Things really started looking up, this one Saturday. They had an All-Mouse Cartoon Festival down at the Bijou, I mean it was nonstop, wall-to-wall Mouse. They had Mickey, they had Mighty, they had that old farmer guy with the rodents that were always getting on his case. We come out of it so full of popcorn and just laughing and slapping and murphing around, I was practically in a good mood.

By the time we got back, it was getting dark; half a dozen dead-end kids were checking out the truck, that we still had parked out front. They knew it was ours and they knew we were guys with guns, so so far they hadn't touched it: but someday that touch would come. For now, I just slapped my palm with a tire-iron and they scattered; but they'd be back. All that H was looking more and more like a liability.

"What say we heft this stuff safe upstairs, good brother, 'fore it up and walks off."

249

We humped the boxes up the stairs, sweaty work. Then we emptied it all out on the pool table, just to see what it would look like all in a heap. Completely covered the surface, several inches deep. I'd practically forgot all about it, but seeing it now all there together, all white and shiny, gave me an idea.

Joey was impressed too, and said sadly, "It's almost a shame we gotta turn it over to the cops."

I shake my head and wince at him. "What's this with you and the cops, Joey? You're always going on about them. Next thing you know you'll be chomping on donuts and wearing a badge."

"Yeh." He grinned. "Run you in for gluttony."

"Yeh right whatever; but the cops got better stuff to do. Like hold the coffee-creamer for the better class of bankers and Napoleons of crime. Why give it away to them and let *them* sell it? No, the way I figure, we're going into business for ourselves."

He steps back, real stiff. "OH no, Murphy. You crossed the line now. I ain't dealing and you ain't either. And no confession scam this time."

"Who said anything about dealin' it? We're gonna just trade it right back to the Mob where it belongs. — Look, we got no use for it; and the street, the street always get what it needs. Sometimes more expensive, sometimes less. More expensive, just means that many more citizens the junkies gotta rob. So we'd be doing the taxpayers a favor."

"Well, trade it for what?"

"For Mallow."

Joey gets this big smile spreading like syrup on the pancake of his face. "Elder brother, you just had yourself an I-dea!"

So the next day I sent a letter to my good buddy Big Tony, with a little baggie in it with smack in it, to show him how pure. I tell him there's a couple tons more where that come from, at reasonable rates. I sign it "Love, Lulu", but I give my real number. Maybe risky, in case he's still ticked off about that other stuff, but at this point I have nothing to lose, in this life or the next.

Real soon, I reckon about ten seconds after the postman makes it across town through the summer sleet to Tony's house, the phone rings.

Not even a 'hello'. Just: "Talk."

"Hey, hiya, Fatso, I mean Biggo. Yep, we got the smack; but me I'm a beer man, mostly, y'know? and it's been hangin heavy on our hands. So if you're innarested, name a time and a place."

"We're interested," he says, ignoring my teasing now that he can smell deal. "The town's starving; only problem is, that'll come to *some* chunk of money, and right now we got a little tickee-washee problem, the small bills aren't back yet from the laundromat. All we got is stuff with an odor, and you wouldn't want that."

"No problem, Tony Big. We're not after jack."

251

There's an amazed silence, if a silence can sound amazed. He attempts to process this. "So what is it that you're after."

"A man."

This sinks in.

"O-kay, that takes us into different territory. Frankly, it's over my level. I gotta go call up the don from Boca Raton. He's planning to be here Saturday evening. At five, we call to tell you where."

"Okey-doke, big Tone. Ciao."

When I hung up, I was happy as a clam in clover. Mallow was so close — I could touch him and taste him. I went and got Joey in the pool-room, where he was playing against the Fates, and said Let's celebrate.

"What's the occasion, Murphy? Piglet have another birthday?"

"No hey, it's our case, remember our case. Celebrate as how we're about to get the total scoop on Mallow, probably meet the man himself."

"Hm. You so sure?"

"It's a cert! Since that shipment slipped out of sight and all the wires got crossed, now the junkies in this city are down to living off Mars bars, praying for the day. That junk in the trunk is now worth more than ever. Heck they'd trade us their grandmothers for it."

"Whaddawe want with a buncha grandmothers? — No right, I getcha: Mallow. But ... you sure they got a line on him?"

"More than a line. It all ties in. He worked with them at one time, might be working with them again. He had some kind of hand or thumb or big toe or something in this shipment we came into. And it was Mallow they were asking about back when they were shaking Willie up and down."

"Well okay, good brother, but don't get your hopes to high, because that way they got farther to fall."

We headed over to our favorite place to celebrate, The El Hoi Polloi Greeko-Espanish Café. They got that good Greek pizza, American-style. There we ran into Sammy, back in form and passing out lapel-pins, and showing the town to a couple of low-rollers, so we all teamed up. Got a booth, and were about to order pitchers but I was feeling too good: we had them just wheel out a keg and leave it next to our table. Joey proposed a toast, and then I did, and then everybody got their licks in. We passed the evening sipping and singing, scarfing and barfing, saying good-bye to the old life.

It was the last day of summer.

***

The crack of dawn came late to us the next day, around mid-afternoon. When I finally got up and showered, I felt as though I was going to be going to a graduation ceremony. Momma (if she'd stuck around) would have been so proud.

Nature had turned down the thermostat a notch, the first faint crisp hints of the autumn that was to come. I put on a t-shirt a shade darker and a ways cleaner than last week's. Joey looked terrific in tank-top and Gumby overalls. Then we put on our bowling jackets, a special occasion.

The phone call came, it's not Tony, another guy, very suave, saying our escorts would be by to pick us up in fifteen minutes. He didn't mention where they would be taking us. And as it turned out, an actual address would've been be difficult to give. Just: Drive till you come to the slums; turn left; head on out through the wastelands till you come to a bunch of rubble, and it's the abandoned factory that has no name. We were glad for the escort service, because the don likes it we be on time.

Right on the dot, the doorbell does its number, and we hustle down the stairs. At the front door are two men in dark suits, they look like they just been pallbearers for somebody's mother.

"Hey, Luigi!" I greet them. "And — why, shut my mouth — it's Squigi! Ronzoni macaroni manicotti ferrari, fellas!"

Don't either one of 'em crack a smile. Maybe it was *their* mother. They just get into their car and disappear behind the tainted glass, driving off slowly with their hazard lights blinking, while me and Joey follow on, in our loaded-up truck.

We finally draw up outside a one-story cinder-block job, maybe useta make crutches or condoms or something. The two guys leave their car unlocked and walk in, not even looking over at us. We park the truck and follow at a respectful distance.

"You nervous, Murphy?" asks Joey out of the side of his mouth.

"Man I been nervous my whole life. I'm just a jumpy guy. This isn't so bad. The worst these jerks can do is kill me, save someone else the trouble. Let's go do it."

We walk in, it's just one big room, filling the entire factory, lit here and there with makeshift lighting. A smell of dust and drywall and flaked concrete. A huge oval table in the center, guys around it with grave faces, like a great big poker game. At the middle of one side, quiet and undemonstrative, sits an older man, in gold-rim bifocals. It's the don — you can tell.

"He-heyy, Donny-boy," I say, but it falls flat, and I let it lie there. Someone motions to some chairs and we sit down, across from the don.

"So," he says, coming right to the point. "Do you have the merchandise?"

"Yep."

"Same as the sample?"

"Roger. Roger Wilco. Test it if you like."

The don motions to a couple of men in lab coats and they go out.

"You sold any of it?"

"None. Negative. We're not in that line of business."

"Good! Very good." All up and down the line on both sides of him, heads are nodding, people murmuring "good, good"; they think it's a swell idea we don't wish to follow in *their* grandfather's footsteps and horn in on their business. See, everybody knows these guys are pretty down on commonism, but when it comes to free enterprise, they really draw the line. They don't laissez anybody faire but their ownsome.

"And I am informed you do not wish cash payment, but instead we deliver you a person."

"Roger, you got it."

The don removes his spectacles and thoughtfully cleans the lenses. "This leads us into a potentially delicate area. Your merchandise is substantial in quantity, and —" the chemists have filtered back in and have nodded an okay "— of exceptional quality. But it would not suffice — this might surprise you — to buy yourselves just anyone. Not, for example, a Supreme Court justice, nor a senior Senator. And even for smaller fry, complications can arise. We need to better understand your motivations; and in particular — since you are obviously not the brains of the operation — who is behind you, who is ordering the hit."

The dime drops. "No you got it all wrong! It's not a hit — we want the man alive!"

256

Heads turn; concerned murmurs. "Very unusual and even more strange. In my own experience, actually unprecedented. What has he done to you?"

"Nothing! We want him alive and well. This isn't a snatch job; the guy just talks to us and then he can walk away."

Gasps around the table. The don exclaims: "A blood relative! One of our long-term guests enjoying our hospitality back in the old country, perhaps. Well, that would depend on what he has done to *us*. And it goes above my level as well. I shall have to place a call back to the Island."

"No no no, it's not like that. He's just some guy; we never even met him."

A general commotion among those present. Are we insane? We're not acting it, plus we strode in here to their hideout, cool as cucumbers, with the finest stash in a long time out in our truck. The don leans over to his right and goes into a huddle, then turns to us.

"Try as I might, I can find no objection. Your motivations are your own. So, who's the party?"

I draw myself up and say it loud and clear. "Richie Mallow."

Stunned silence. The don again takes off his reading glasses and stares. "For … Richie *Mallow*?! For — What are you, some kind of *morons*? You just escape from some kind, some variety of *home*? **We iced Mallow three months ago, in Corsica!!!**"

The words float out into the air like smoke from a fine cigar — like bits of confetti, dancing in the light — confetti from a party, a classy tony party, maybe on Wall Street, early October 1929. A loud and happy party, with prizes and funny hats, where everybody at it had died long ago. Now fluttering down, down, down ... like dead moths.

All the oxygen has gone out of the room. I gasp for breath. Then I turn to Joey and say softly, "We blew it, brother." He hangs his head.

The don has now lit a cigar to help calm him down, and he's waving it. "Look, I'm really sorry about this, didn't know he was a friend of yours. But you, in *our* place? You'd've done the same thing. He was two-timing his buddies that know him from a child. Dealing stuff on the side, stuff that didn't belong to him. It just wasn't ethical."

I nodded. "I understand."

And now the guy really is sorry. I just look so lost. "Look — here — I'll find out if anybody held on to his jacket or his wallet or anything like that. They might have — there was no widow. — Hey, see to it, okay, Charlie?"

The chappie in question nods.

But then he turns stern. "Only ... We still do want that horse, you know." A little hard edge forms around the outlines of his voice.

"Yeh sure, a deal's a deal," I say in a dull voice. "We'll even throw in the truck. Not that many miles on it, and a tank half full of gas. You kept your end of the bargain, you told me what I needed to know. And yeh sure, send his stuff on, if there is any, why not. I'll keep it as a souvenir."

For a moment the don seems almost embarrassed, at a loss for what to say. But then he becomes expansive. "A pleasure to do business with you, gentlemen! And hey, anytime! Maybe some favors we can do you someday. You want some cash? Laundered cleaner than a Father's collar. You want broads? Carefully inspected, also clean. Just name it."

I sigh and shake my head. "No, thanks, that's okay. We'll call it even. C'mon, Joey, let's go home."

We get up heavily, jackets slung over our shoulder. But then Joey has a sudden inspiration. "Wait, Murphy, remember — the teevee! Maybe these guys could get it out of hock for us."

"Hm, yeh, well, right now, don't really feel like watchin' TV."

"Yeh, guess you're right. There's nothing good on."

"So I guess that's it, then." I give the guys a weak little wave as we leave. "Thanks for everything. So long."

Nobody stops us. The drivers who led us here step forward to offer us a lift, but we wave them off, we'd rather just walk. And so we head slowly back home, heavy of tread, heavy of heart.

It's a long long walk, takes us most of the night. Our feet are tired. It's Sunday, dawn dawning, the buses have stopped running. We're walking in silence up the empty sidewalks, back from the docks, on the long way home.

After a mile and a while, we're coming up to a little parish church — one window still lit, like it's been lit all night — lit all my life. Joey gets ready to follow me crossing to the far side of the street — what we've been doing since we started in feeling so bad; but I hold him back. "No, Joey, not this time." He pauses and turns, patiently, wordlessly waiting what thing I might say.

"See Joey I been thinking. What started this case, and all the stuff that we done." I shiver; the air is maybe mild but I feel cold. "I think of what I done, knowing I was doing it. And what it all came out to. And now — and now I'm sorry, Joey." I feel so cold. "I am really, truly sorry, Joey." I look up at the grey stone walls of the old church, rising from the sad stained sidewalk as though soaring, or imploring.

"But you know what? If ever I did blaspheme the Holy Ghost, — you know that I did not mean it. And the *Ghost* knows. I just got this feeling —" again the shiver of chill —"*I am squared with the Ghost, and the Ghost is not sore.*"

Again a gaze at the old church door — a gaze once wistful, but now determined.

"I'm going in."

~ ~ ~

So there you have it, all wrapped up and topped with a bow: the Case of the Heisted Heroin; or, Murphy and the Seven Hoods — call it whatever you like. For me it'll always be simply the Case of a Wrong Guy and a Wronged Dame.

So I wrote up my report, like always, and submitted my bill. The bill said simply, "Call it even"; and there was no client to read the report. So I folded it up and sealed it in a bottle; then I went down to the docks, and hurled it out as far and as far as I might, out into the deep salt sea. Where it will float out with the current, and be chivvied by the sharp chill winds, and drift — we know not whither, it is out of our hands. And yet by grace of Him who shaped the deep, and Who rules it with His wide quiet hand, it yet may find a port someday, when its time has finally arrived. — And this, at last, has happened: for here you are, reading this, poring over these lines, so many years after I first wrote them, so long after these things happened here on Earth.

So go well, to become what you in time may be, within His keeping; or to your final rest, if this be now what is required of you, after your long life; to that which awaits us — thee, and me; and in this, as in all things, Bless.

www.ingramcontent.com/pod-product-compliance
Lightning Source LLC
Chambersburg PA
CBHW072208170626
46813CB00003B/839